Haunted Hair Nights

Nancy J. Cohen

HAUNTED HAIR NIGHTS
Copyright © 2016 by Nancy J. Cohen
Published by Orange Grove Press

Digital ISBN: 978-0-9970038-3-3
Print ISBN: 978-0-9970038-4-0
Cover Design by http://boulevardphotografica.yolasite.com/
Digital Layout by www.formatting4U.com

This is a work of fiction. Names, characters, places, and incidents either are the product of the author's imagination or are used fictitiously, and any resemblance to actual persons, business establishments, events or locales is entirely coincidental.

All rights reserved. This book is licensed for your personal use only. No part of this work may be used, reproduced, stored in an information retrieval system, or transmitted in any form or by any means (electronic, mechanical, photocopying, recording, or otherwise) without prior written consent by the author. Any usage of the text, except for brief quotations embodied in critical articles or reviews, without the author's permission is a violation of copyright.

Haunted Hair Nights

Chapter One

"I don't know why I let you talk me into helping your class plan a haunted house for Halloween," Marla said, her gaze focused on the road. Dense trees lined the pothole-riddled street as she drove down a narrow two-lane drive barely lit by sparse streetlamps. Twilight had descended, and she didn't relish returning this way in the dark. Who would live in this remote location west of Fort Lauderdale and nearly at the Everglades?

Brianna glanced at her with an eager expression. "You'll enjoy tonight, Marla. I'm counting on you to fix the mannequins' hair so they look scary."

The high schooler had forsaken her usual ponytail to wear her dark brown hair in soft curls. Marla wondered if she were trying to impress someone in particular. Brianna hadn't mentioned any boys to her and Dalton, but Marla had overheard her in conversation with friends. The name Andy popped up often.

Dalton hadn't noticed, thank goodness. Her husband had enough trouble accepting his fifteen-year-old daughter nearing college age. Worrying about the young men she might be attracting would send him into the stratosphere.

"I'll do my best," Marla replied. "But as much as I like to experiment on the mannequin heads in my salon, I'm not sure how I can contribute to your class project."

"Any help will be appreciated."

Marla heard the petulant note in her stepdaughter's voice. She'd been a reluctant volunteer. Parenting didn't come naturally to her, and since marrying Dalton, she hadn't rushed into school-related activities like other moms. Coming tonight was a big concession on her part, but she'd wanted to please her new family.

And it was a good thing she had come, considering this place's isolated location. "Who picked this site? Do you really think the parents from your school would drive their kids all the way out here?"

"Mr. Ripari offered it to us. Although he's never lived there, the house has been in his family since the 1940s."

"He's your history teacher, right?"

Brianna nodded. "This location is creepy. It'll be perfect."

Oh, yeah, maybe if you're in a slasher movie. Marla didn't have a good feeling about their adventure. She wondered why Dalton, a homicide detective, had given his approval.

A number of other cars were parked in a trampled grass lot to the side of the house. Bright lights beckoned to them from inside the two-story residence as Marla pulled into a vacant space. She shut down the ignition and waited for the headlights to switch off.

As she emerged into the warm October air, she wondered if they'd get the promised cold front in time for Halloween. She stepped carefully toward the sprawling house, not wishing to encounter any fire ants in her low-heeled sandals. An enormous tree shaded this side of the place. Judging from its thick trunk, the thing must be hundreds of years old.

"Look at that," she said to Brianna, who made a game of identifying trees in nature parks with her dad. "Can you believe how far those branches spread?"

"It's a kapok tree," Brianna replied in a superior tone. "It's so cool that Mr. Ripari is letting us use this property for our fundraiser. The house looks downright spooky in this setting."

Marla admired the old Florida architecture as she climbed a short flight of creaky wooden steps onto a wraparound covered porch. The jalousie-type windows at this level were partially secured with crisscrossed boards, poor protection against hurricanes. This place would cost a fortune to bring up to code. Why did the history teacher keep the property if he couldn't maintain it?

Brianna scampered ahead and banged open the front door. Marla followed, a sea of faces glancing her way as she stepped inside. The teen called out a greeting to kids she knew and then seemed to recollect Marla's presence. She turned to introduce her.

Marla would never remember everyone's names. A dozen people must have been present, all occupied with sorting through a ton of supplies. The gang of busy workers had materials strewn everywhere. Fake cobwebs, rubber spiders, bony skeletons, glow sticks, and other goods covered several work tables, while cartons cluttered the floor. Sheet-covered furniture lent an authenticity to the scene, as did grimy chandeliers.

"Hi, I'm Bill Ripari," said a broad-chested man with spiky black hair and eyeglasses. He wore a friendly smile and a sheen of sweat on his forehead.

"Nice to meet you." Marla shook his hand. "It's generous of you to offer your property for the haunted house."

"Might as well get some use out of the old girl. She's been deserted for years."

"Such a shame. I imagine this place was beautiful in its heyday."

He drew her aside and lowered his voice. "I'm hoping to preserve the house as a piece of our region's history."

"You've applied to get it on the state's register of historic homes?"

"Actually, I'm in talks with a company that owns a popular theme park in Orlando. They're looking for a property to the south."

"You mean to sell the estate then?"

"Don't worry; any offer has to come with the agreement to renovate this house authentic to the time period. I'd like to see it reopened as a living history museum."

"When was the original purchase?" she asked, realizing some of Dalton's interest in history must have rubbed off on her.

"My grandfather bought the territory in 1942. He built this house on an agricultural tract. In the late 1950s, he leased the acreage to folks who turned it into a pioneer theme park, with the caveat that the house be preserved. The park closed in 1964. At that time, my dad tore down the tourist attractions and converted the original house into a restaurant. It remained in business until he died. The place has been closed ever since then."

"And you hung onto it all this time?"

"I knew the value of the land would increase. I own much of the woods out here as well as the house. It will be perfect for the Orlando company's planned expansion, as long as they honor my wishes."

"It sounds like a good compromise, if they don't tear down these woods in the process. And I'm not sure we need any thrill rides out this way. You can take an airboat in the Everglades for that experience."

He guffawed. "I like you, lady. I'm thinking more like a recreated village from the past."

"That would work."

"I think so." The history teacher glanced at a tall, lanky fellow in a gray uniform who lugged a bucket along with a handful of Styrofoam. "Mr. Lynch, please don't track that dirt in here. You'll have to clean your shoes before you go upstairs."

"Yes, Mr. Ripari." The fellow gave a respectful nod and turned toward the rear.

"Tom is our school janitor. He's earning some extra money by helping us out," Mr. Ripari explained. He patted his ample belly, his green sport shirt hanging over his pants. "Physical labor isn't my thing. Since my repair skills are limited, I'm planning to hire Tom as a handyman in his spare time once this project is finished."

"Don't monopolize the lady, Bill," called one of the women volunteers. The blonde had a harried look on her face. "She can assist us over here."

"Sure," Marla said with a wave in her direction. "How big is this place, anyway?"

"The upper level has twelve rooms," Mr. Ripari replied. "Down here, six sections had been converted into dining rooms for the restaurant, plus the kitchen. Unfortunately, most of the restaurant furnishings were sold, along with furniture from the earlier residence. It's a shame, but this is all that's left. More stuff is stored in the detached garage and in various corners throughout the house. I'd been hoping to sort through it all when I retired, but that won't happen anytime soon."

"This would make a great retirement home with all its rooms," Marla mused aloud. "But the restoration would cost a fortune, plus an elevator would have to be added."

"There's a dumb waiter by the kitchen. That space could be converted, but this site is too far from civilization for an old age home. As a historic house museum and native Florida attraction, it would be perfect. Thanks for coming to help. Your daughter is a lovely girl, by the way. I enjoy having her in my class." He nodded at Brianna, engaged in conversation with a young man.

"Thank you. She's not too keen on world history, but she likes reading about our state. My husband is more of a general history buff."

"Is that so? Too bad he couldn't join us tonight. Now if

you'll excuse me, I have work to do on the graveyard outside."

Marla wandered over to the teen. Brianna gave her a guilty flush at her arrival.

"Marla, this is Andrew Lawrence. He and I are in math class together. Andy, meet my stepmom."

This must be the Andy whose name she'd heard Brianna mention. She examined the kid, who was cute even to someone of her age. He stood taller than Brianna, with a thick head of sandy hair and intelligent brown eyes. "Hello, Andrew. Have you worked on these haunted house projects before?"

"No, ma'am. Brie talked me into volunteering. She can be persuasive."

"That's for sure. Do you have plans for college? The time to apply will be here before you know it."

He gave a nervous chuckle. "I'd like to go to MIT."

"Oh, really? What will you study?"

"I'm hoping to get into robotics. It's a field that's always fascinated me."

"That's cool." Marla glanced at Brianna, who was studiously examining the floor. "Brie would like to attend a school in the Boston area, too. She says she's tired of Florida."

The blond woman interrupted their tête-à-tête. "Hi, I'm Hannah," she said to Marla. "We could use your help if you're not busy."

"Okay. Nice to meet you," Marla told Andrew. She turned away, suddenly aware of how grown up Brianna looked with her hair down and a light application of makeup on her face. From the way Andy had been sneaking glances at her, he'd noticed also.

"That's my son Ricky over there." Hannah pointed to a tall, gangly kid busy cutting a piece of white cloth. "So you're Brianna's mom?"

"I'm her stepmother, actually. It's a second marriage for her dad and me."

"I'm sure she appreciates you getting involved in school activities."

This is my first time, Marla almost said but didn't. "I hope you'll guide me. I have no concept of what a haunted house entails, other than decorations from the party store."

"It'll be fabulous. Jules, can you bring up the layout design on your computer?" she asked a youth fixing a gruesome monster mask onto a long stick. He had a pasty complexion and owlish eyes as though he didn't get out much.

"Sure, our plan is awesome." Jules toddled over to a laptop and accessed a screen showing the house's two-story diagram. "This is where guests will enter through the front porch," he told Marla. "We'll have a mummy sitting on this bench here, a couple of cheesecloth ghosts, spider webs, and the graveyard out on the lawn. The windows are partially boarded up, which helps our cause, and our paper cutouts will add to the spooky atmosphere as people approach. Tickets will be on sale at a booth on the front porch."

Marla squinted at the screen. "How can you control where people walk when they come inside?"

He shifted his feet back and forth, as though he couldn't stand still. "We'll be partitioning this space where you are now, so they'll have to follow along a planned path. See this spot? It's what we call a scare pocket."

"What's that?" Marla stared at the diagram in confusion. This undertaking was a lot more complex than she'd expected.

"It's where an actor pops out and scares people. We've got some students from a local acting class to volunteer." Jules proceeded to explain the route and the various decorations along the way. He spoke rapidly as though wired on caffeine, and accompanied his speech with jerky motions.

She glanced at the stairway that guests would have to climb. "How do you know this place is safe? I mean, nobody has lived here for years. People could trip on the carpet, or one of your fake walls could fall down. Candles could tip over. Is there even air-conditioning?"

"Yes, the house has wall units. It hasn't been modernized with a central system, but those are enough to filter the air," Hannah reassured her. "Besides, we won't have any real candles. We've bought the fake ones with flickering flames. We'll also have a fog machine, and dry ice is another technique we use to provide smoke."

"How so?" Marla had no clue about these things.

Hannah gave her a patient smile, while Marla felt totally out of the loop. "You fill bowls, glassware, and jars with warm water. Right before we open the doors, we'll add dry ice to get everything bubbling. Between black lights, glow sticks, fake candles, and lanterns, we'll create the right atmosphere. It's Mr. Lynch's job to make sure there aren't any wrinkles in the carpet, loose floorboards, or nails sticking out."

Marla lifted her eyebrows. She didn't want to ask if they had liability insurance, but maybe Mr. Ripari's homeowners' policy covered the event. Or more likely, the school purchased extra coverage for sponsored activities like this one.

"What are you working on?" she asked.

Hannah dragged her toward a high-top table. "See these cardboard tubes? I'm cutting out eyes in them. We put glow sticks inside. Same deal for the monster shapes over there. We tape them to the windows so people can see them as they walk up to the house. My son is doing the cheesecloth ghosts for the graveyard."

Marla pointed to another woman, who appeared to be spraying an object with white paint. Newspapers lined the floor underneath her project. "What's she doing?"

"Vicki is spraying dolls with white paint. It looks hugely creepy when you sit them on the covered furniture or stand them in a corner and shine a light on them from below. We also have some plaster statues left over from the early days that we can use, as well as the mannequins we brought in."

"Brie said you wanted me to work on their hair?"

"Yes, they're over here." She led Marla to a corner where the figures were stacked.

Marla assessed them with her practiced eye. "I have a kit in my car. I'll go get it and start working on these."

She went outside, retrieved her "backstage box" with hairdressing supplies, and reentered the house. "So have you worked on this school project before?" she asked Hannah as they toiled side-by-side in the large room. Marla teased the hair on a mannequin to give it a frightful look. Too bad she didn't have any spray-on hair color. That would have worked well under the right lighting. She'd have to remember to bring some next time.

Hannah pursed her lips. "Yes, this event is our big fundraiser for the prom. It's been in a different location each year, but if this one works out, maybe we can repeat it here again. However, I won't sign on to help unless Mr. Ripari does better by my son."

Marla heard the bitter note in her voice but didn't pry. "The history teacher said he might sell the property, so this could be the one and only time it's available."

"Is that so? I didn't think he could do that, not when his ownership is being challenged. But maybe he's solved that problem."

"What do you mean?"

Hannah glanced over her shoulder before leaning forward. "Rumor says another family is claiming this property belongs to them. They've taken steps to delay a sale until they can present proof."

"That's interesting. Who are they?"

"Hannah, there you are," a male voice boomed from the entry before the other parent could respond. A hefty guy entered carrying a bulging carton. "I've brought your box of plastic weapons."

"Doug, it's about time you showed up. Marla, this is our esteemed football coach. Doug Garsen, meet Marla Vail. She's Brianna's mother."

"Hey, thanks for coming to help us out. Where do you want these?" he asked Hannah, waving a fake axe in the air as though to demonstrate its use.

"Put them in the creature room. What's that on your boots?"

He glanced at the red stains on his footwear. "I spilled a container of fake blood. The stuff is wicked." He set his carton down and grabbed a paper towel from a roll on a work table along with a spray bottle of cleaning fluid.

"Go into the bathroom, will you? You're ruining those newspapers."

After he clomped away, Marla went back to work. She tackled another mannequin, weaving the hair into snake-like coils. Others came and went through various rooms as she concentrated on her artistry. Brianna had disappeared somewhere upstairs.

Eventually, Marla had to use the rest room and asked for directions.

"It's down that hallway, on the same side as the garage," a female student told her. She'd been wrapping mummy tape around one of the mannequins. The girl, whose name was Rose, had taken a long break earlier, making Marla wonder if she'd gone off for a secret smoke or a rendezvous with one of the boys instead of a bathroom visit.

Marla located the facilities, grateful to find a supply of toilet paper if not paper towels. Her face looked tired as she gazed at herself in the mirror. No wonder; she'd been at work all day. After fixing a quick dinner at home, she'd hopped in the car with Brianna to come here.

At least tomorrow was her late day at the salon. On Thursdays, she worked from one to eight, so she'd have the morning free.

Haunted Hair Nights

As she emerged from the lavatory, Marla glanced out a side window on the opposite end of the house from where she'd been working. The darkening sky made it hard to see, but was that a trail of blood leading into the woods?

Oh, how clever. Doug the football coach must have tossed some of his red paint out there, the same stuff he'd gotten on his shoes. Or maybe he'd hosed it off outside, and some of the residue had stained the dirt.

Driven by curiosity, she stepped outdoors through a nearby exit. A coppery scent wafted her way. Wait, wasn't the graveyard in front of the house? That's where their outdoor lighting would be aimed. So why would kids want to come back here in the dark?

Then again, that could be the reasoning for this attraction. A big splotch of the red stuff stained a clump of grass and then dribbled off into the woods. What lay in wait? A pop-up zombie? A shredded cheesecloth ghost? A grasping plaster statue? Or a creepy doll with whitened eyes?

Steeling her nerves, she withdrew a small flashlight from her cross-body purse and inched forward. Slivers of ice pricked her spine as she followed the trail. Somebody had to test the scare zone to see if it worked, right?

Broken tree branches and crushed leaves attested to someone's passage. She stopped at a curve, where thick foliage hid a view of the path ahead. All was still except for leaves rustling and the rapid pounding of her heart. Over there, she thought, her pulse racing. A patch of green showed through the shrubbery.

As she rounded the corner and saw what lay across the trail, she clapped a hand to her mouth.

The green color wasn't grass, and the crumpled form on the ground wasn't a fake dummy meant to enthrall guests.

Her stomach heaved, but she forced the contents down. She stared transfixed, unable to move, as though being still could reverse time and alter the course of events. But nothing would change the fate of the man who lay under a sprinkling of fallen leaves.

Mr. Ripari rested in peace face-up on the ground, dead as the restaurant that had closed its doors. In his gut was a knife that had nothing to do with props and everything to do with death. The grim reaper had arrived, and it was horribly real.

"Help! I need help out here!" She turned and ran toward the house.

Chapter Two

"Tell me again how you managed to stumble upon another murder victim," Dalton said, hours later in their brightly lit kitchen at home. He'd been wonderfully supportive ever since she'd summoned him with a frantic phone call, but now he wanted some answers in private.

Marla, bone weary, sagged into her chair. Brianna had closeted herself in her room, too affected by the death of her teacher to want to discuss it. Making things worse had been the lengthy interview by a police detective who suspected them all. This case wasn't in Dalton's jurisdiction, so he'd had to stand clear.

"It could have been anyone," Marla replied, her hands cupping the mug of coffee he'd made for her. If this disaster didn't put gray into her chestnut hair, she didn't know what else would. "People came and went out of the room where I worked. Brie was upstairs. Some of the kids worked on a graveyard out front."

"So how did the history teacher end up getting knifed in the backyard?"

"Maybe he was meeting someone back there, or he wanted a moment of quiet. How should I know?"

"I can't believe this would happen at a school event where you two were present."

"Let's not start, Dalton. We've been over this. It's not our fault, and we're both safe."

"All right. Let's see what we know about it. The sooner this case is solved, the better I'll feel about Brianna's safety." He stooped to pet Lucky, their golden retriever, who'd nudged him for attention along with Spooks, their cream-colored poodle.

"Bill Ripari owned the place, which he planned to sell to a theme park company from Orlando." Marla related the property's history.

"So who inherits it now?" Dalton asked.

"He wasn't married. One of the parents mentioned that another family was claiming ownership and trying to prevent a sale until they could present proof."

"You don't know who they are? I could check court records for injunctions."

"Also see if Mr. Ripari had filed a will," Marla suggested. "He would have named a beneficiary."

"Good idea." Dalton gave her a thoughtful glance. "Being stabbed with a knife in the middle of a school event indicates a crime of passion. Did anyone there have reason to resent the teacher?"

Marla rubbed a hand over her face. "I've been over this with Detective Hanson. Let's give it a rest for the night. I'm too tired to think anymore, and I feel bad for Brie. She liked Mr. Ripari."

"It appears not everybody shared her sentiment."

His wry tone stuck in her mind as she rose to check on the teen. Brianna lay in bed, staring into space, the sheet pulled up to her chin.

"How could he be dead?" the girl said when Marla entered her room.

Marla sat on the side of her bed and stroked her arm. "I'm so sorry. It was generous of him to offer his house for your event. He seemed like a nice man."

"He was a good teacher. History isn't my favorite subject, but he made it interesting."

What's worse is someone you know might have done it. "They'll find whoever is responsible. Try to get some sleep. We'll all be able to think more clearly in the morning."

Brianna clutched her hand. "You'll help track down the killer, won't you? I'm not going to feel safe at school until we catch the guy."

"*You* will have no part in this. I can talk to the other parents involved, but we have to let the police do their work."

As she prepared for bed, Marla knew she'd get involved. A few inquiries here and there couldn't hurt, under the guise of aiding the students. She made a mental to-do list of people to interview. Her first stop would be the school to offer her condolences and to snoop out any gossip about the deceased teacher.

***

Marla followed the routine for checking into the school. She got a visitor badge from the front office along with the information that grief counselors were available to students regarding poor Mr. Ripari's untimely demise.

"I was there," she confided to Connie the desk clerk, choosing a quiet moment when classes were in session. "Brianna and I were setting up the place for the sophomore class's haunted house. Now it's turned into a real one."

The sixtyish woman gave her a sad smile. "Everyone is upset. Mr. Ripari was well liked by his students and our teachers."

"Will there be a memorial service?"

"I have no idea. He didn't have any relatives to our knowledge, and he was single. We'd all like to attend if there is one."

"It's a shame if the haunted house is cancelled, although that would be appropriate under the circumstances. Could the project be moved, if the class wants to continue it elsewhere?"

"Oh, I doubt anyone will have the heart for it now. And Mr. Ripari's place was perfect, from what I've heard. It's too late in the season to book a site elsewhere."

"What are you saying about Mr. Ripari?" said a stern male voice from behind.

"I was telling Mrs. Vail that we're distraught over his unexpected death, Mr. Underwood," Connie said in a meek tone.

Marla spun around to regard the school principal. "I'm sorry for your school's loss. I thought I'd touch base because Brianna and I were there last night, and we're both still struggling to accept what's happened. If I can help in any way—"

"Come into my office. You can share the details of what you remember." Mr. Underwood signaled for her to follow. "I can't conceive of how Bill was killed with our students present. Why, it could have been one of them! And then imagine the liability case to follow."

"Yes, we don't want any legal ramifications, do we?" Marla trailed him into his private enclave and took a seat after he'd shut the door.

"Please refrain from being facetious. We have to be concerned about these things."

"You're right. Actually, I noticed the house could use some repairs. Did you visit the place before approving it for a school function?"

Mr. Underwood shoved his fingers through his thinning dark hair. The color was a bit too uniformly dark to be natural. "Of course. Bill promised to fix things up to ensure the kids' safety. He wouldn't have received permission otherwise."

"I understand he meant to sell the property. Did you know it had been a tourist attraction back in the early days? Another theme park company is interested in acquiring the land. Mr. Ripari said any sale would be contingent upon the buyer converting the house into a living history museum. He envisioned the site as a recreated village from the past. However, I've heard there's some controversy over the ownership."

The principal gave a dismissive wave. "It's no secret. He was quite incensed that another family was trying to claim inheritance rights."

"How is that even possible?"

"They're saying a secret marriage occurred, and half the property should belong to their family."

"And this has only come to light now?"

"I believe a certain diary was found. It must have mentioned this wedding."

"Who are these people? Do you have any clue?"

"It isn't my affair, Mrs. Vail. I'm merely sharing the concerns Bill expressed to me. So who all did you meet at the house last night?"

Marla described the people who'd helped on the project. "Do you know anyone among them who might have held a grudge against your history teacher?"

He gave a furtive glance at the door and lowered his voice. "I shouldn't say this, but you're married to that police detective, right? It might be important to the case. One of the mothers has been in here a few times complaining about Bill's grading system. She's afraid if her son fails his class, it'll hurt Ricky's chances of getting into the college of her choice."

"*Her* choice?" Marla repeated, not dissuading him of the notion that her husband would be involved in the investigation.

"Yes, she's one of *those* moms." His face brightened with a happy grin meant to disarm. "You're great with Brianna, by the way. She raves about you. You're a good role model for her."

"Why, thank you, Mr. Underwood. I do my best."

He ushered her out, while she wondered what nuggets of information she'd contributed to their dialogue. From her viewpoint, he'd offered two leads to follow. One involved the family trying to edge in on Mr. Ripari's inheritance, and the other suggested an overachieving mother. The name, Ricky, rang a bell. Wasn't this Hannah's son from last night?

She stopped by the front desk again, giving Connie a sweet smile. "Is there any way I could get a copy of the ladies belonging to the parent-teacher association? I may need to contact some of the moms about our project."

"Are you a member? We usually give out a roster at the beginning of the year."

"I've joined, so my name should be listed. I couldn't come to the first meeting." *Or the next few meetings after that one.* She had to try harder hereafter. "Thanks," she added after Connie handed over a booklet. "Can you let me know if there's a memorial for Mr. Ripari? Maybe the school will do something if no one else steps forward."

"We should, especially since the school might benefit from his death." Connie's face reddened. "Oops, I shouldn't have said that."

Another woman entered and strode directly to the principal's office, where she knocked on his door. After she disappeared inside, Marla leaned inward toward the desk clerk.

"Exactly how will the school benefit from Mr. Ripari's death?" Maybe he wasn't as well liked as Mr. Underwood let on. In that case, the other teachers might have been hoping for a replacement.

"Look, this doesn't go beyond these doors, but poor Bill told us that since he had no close relations, he'd left us a bequest in his will. The properties he owned would go into a trust for the school should anything bad happen to him."

Haunted Hair Nights

Chapter Three

Marla left the administrative suite and strode down a long hallway, her shoes tapping on the vinyl flooring. Closed doors on either side indicated classes in session. The odor of wax polish mixed with the smell of old gym socks. It brought back memories of Marla's high school days and her ambitions to become a teacher. She remembered the angst of wanting to be accepted into the popular crowd and winning favor by doing girls' hair. It took two years of college to reveal her true calling. She hadn't done hair to ingratiate herself into a clique. She'd enjoyed creating works of hair art and making women look good in the process.

Speaking of looking good, this place needed renovations. The linoleum flooring was gouged in spots. The paint needed refreshing, and cracks in the ceiling could use repair. She and Dalton had attended Brianna's functions here. How come she'd never noticed these details before?

Connie's words rang in her ears as she headed toward the gym to interview the football coach. So the school would benefit from Mr. Ripari's demise if nobody else's claim on his property proved valid. What if somebody had hastened the teacher's death before he could sell the land? Someone like Principal Underwood, whose reputation would shine should such a bonus land in his school's lap.

Marla believed one of the volunteers from that night must have murdered the man, but she could be wrong. Another person might have lured the history teacher outside.

She pushed open the double doors into the gym. The thump of a ball bouncing and the sound of teens yelling told her a basketball game was in session even before her eyes registered the action. A coach's whistle blew loudly and often, but he wasn't the man she sought.

"Where can I find Coach Garsen?" she asked the nearest youth, a pimply-faced kid.

"Check his office. It's past the boys' locker room in that direction."

"Okay, thanks." Marla paced forward, keeping to the edge of the gym and out of range of the game in progress.

As she passed the locker room, voices drifted her way through the partially open door.

"Did you tell Coach Garsen?" one boy said, his deep tone indicating his older age.

"Hell, no, man. I don't want him to cut my supply."

"You're sick. You should let him know. It could get worse."

"It'll be worse for me if I get kicked off the team. He'll stop giving me the pills, and then I'll fall behind."

Pills? Marla paused, tilting her head to hear better and praying no one spotted her there.

"You won't get a scholarship if people find out, and that could put the rest of us at risk. I'm gonna tell him if you don't, Benny."

"You keep your mouth shut, man. I'll deal with it."

A gravelly male voice intruded. "Why are you boys lingering in here? Get your sorry asses back to class."

"Yes, Mr. Lynch," said the older kid with a sneer in his tone.

They must have shuffled off, because for a moment silence reigned. Marla prepared to vamoose if she heard the janitor's footsteps coming her way. Instead, metal clanged on metal inside the locker room. She pushed the door open another crack and dared to peek in. The lanky maintenance

Haunted Hair Nights

man stood in front of an open locker, an intent look on his face as he rummaged through the contents.

What was he doing? Saving her questions about his behavior for later, Marla hurried past, not wishing to get caught snooping. At an office labeled Faculty Only, she knocked on the door. When nobody answered, she twisted the knob. It opened easily. Inside, papers covered nearly every surface, but she was glad to see a personal touch. Potted plants provided happy contrast to the gray institutional monotony. Graphs and charts depicting teams and schedules hung on the walls. To a non-sports fan like herself, they were completely indecipherable.

The coach emerged from his inner office, a pencil tucked behind his ear. "Hello, how can I help you?"

"I'm Marla Vail, Brianna's mother. We met at the haunted house."

He hung his head, no small feat considering the beefy weight of it. "Sad business, wasn't it? I still can't believe we've lost Mr. Ripari. The kids all liked him."

"Did they? Do you have a minute to chat, Coach? I have a few concerns about my daughter's safety." *Not to mention those pills the kid mentioned, but we'll let that go for now.*

"Sure, ma'am, although I'm not clear on what I can do for you. Come inside."

She sat in a chair opposite the desk. Framed certificates decorated the walls, while gleaming trophies filled the bookshelves. A splash of sunlight came from a window overlooking the parking lot.

"So do you teach classes in addition to coaching the football team?" she asked, trying to discern his role.

"Yes, I'm on the physical education staff." He fingered a coffee mug on his desk.

"You've been with the school a long time?"

"Ten years. What's on your mind, Mrs. Vail?"

Marla clasped her hands in her lap and dove in. "I'll get

to the point. A man was murdered at a school-sponsored event. Stabbed to death. It troubles me how you arrived with red stains on your boots that night."

"It was fake blood. We've used it all the time in our haunted houses."

"So you'd said. How does one tell the difference? I mean, if the cops used Luminol, would they see your footprints coming into the house?"

"What's that?"

"Luminol is a substance used to detect blood spatter at crime scenes. I imagine it would distinguish between real blood and the fake stuff."

"Mr. Lynch cleaned the floor. Why don't you ask him how easily it mopped up?"

"I might do so. How did you get on with Bill Ripari?"

His lips flattened, and his brows drew together. "I don't see why that's any of your business."

"My daughter's security at this school is my concern. The sooner the killer is caught, the more we can all rest easy. Doesn't it make you uncomfortable that a man died on our watch, so to speak?"

"Do you think it doesn't bother me? It's hard to know who to trust around here."

"Your students must trust you, Coach. Football can be a tough sport. Lots of injuries and bruised egos. You need boys with enough physical strength to keep up."

"Tell me something I don't know. Where are you going with this?"

"It's always possible Mr. Ripari discovered something going on at the school that might be cause for dismissal of either a student or a faculty member."

He leapt to his feet. "I hope you're not implying that I—"

"Of course not, but a couple of those students might have had reason to resent him. Like, were there any kids failing his class who might have held a grudge?"

Haunted Hair Nights

He gazed at her in a more thoughtful manner. "You might be onto something. There's a couple...nah, I shouldn't say anything."

"Please, Coach," she said in a sugary tone. "You'd be helping the school catch a killer. That will make things safer for everyone."

"Since you've mentioned it, we have one kid on our team who shied away every time Bill Ripari passed by. Patrick has some problems, but he's a good boy."

"Where can I find him?"

"It's Patrick Evans, but you didn't hear it from me. And don't mention this to your cop husband, either. We don't need him snooping around here and upsetting people. Patrick hangs out at Dee's Diner after school. He likes their chocolate milkshakes."

"Okay. Anybody else?"

The coach seemed willing to cast suspicion on others, perhaps to distract her from his own activities that were less than legal.

"Nope. I shouldn't have said even this much." He gestured toward the open door. "If you don't mind, I have to get back to work."

She got the hint and rose. "Thanks, Coach. If you think of anything else, please give me a call. I've helped my husband solve cases before. Here's my card with my phone numbers."

Outside the office, she almost ran into Mr. Lynch, busy dusting the blinds on a series of windows overlooking the athletic field. Had he heard their conversation?

"Hi, we met at the haunted house last night," she told him. "Do you have a minute to answer a few questions? Mr. Garsen says you cleaned up those boot prints he tracked into the place. Is red paint that easy to wipe away?"

His sharp blue eyes regarded her. He had a tanned face under a head of dark hair, making her wonder when he spent time outdoors. "It ain't paint, miss," he said in a subservient tone that seemed in contrast to his quiet confidence. "You can buy fake blood at the party store. It mops up clean and easy."

"Have you been working for the school a long time?"

"I've been here for two years, miss. Times have changed since I were in high school."

"Tell me about it. Some places have guards patrolling their hallways. Maybe this school needs one. Do you think the students are in any danger from the person who killed the history teacher? My daughter's safety is at stake."

"Is that why you be talking to the coach?" He gave her a hard stare that raised the hairs on the back of her neck.

"He's the one who tramped in with red stains on his shoes shortly before Mr. Ripari's dead body was found."

"You're the lady who found the poor gent, ain't you?"

"Yes, and it was horrible. I can't help wondering who might have hated him enough to shove a knife in his chest."

"Could be lots of folks." Mr. Lynch gripped his duster, glancing at the blinds as though eager to get back to his menial task. Or was he looking away because he had a motive to hide?

"Do you have someone particular in mind? I've heard Mr. Ripari was well-liked by his students."

"Not all of them. He might have appeared like the right sort, but he weren't a saint. He owned stolen property, he did."

"Who else would want that piece of land out in the middle of nowhere?"

"That be a big house, and it has historic value. Plus, the land itself is worth plenty."

The bell rang. Any minute, the hall would be invaded by hordes of students. Marla rushed her final question. "The principal mentioned that another family might have a viable claim on it."

The janitor regarded her with a peculiar light in his eyes.

"Rumor says Mr. Ripari's uncle was secretly married to one of the Conroy gals. The house should rightfully pass to her kin." With those words, he turned away to resume his job.

Doors slammed open, and high schoolers poured into the hallway. Marla jostled her way toward the exit, hearing snatches of conversation that made her glad to be long gone from this phase of her life. She'd never again want to return to the insecurity of her teen years.

Marla signed out at the front office and returned her visitor's badge. Once outside, she heaved a sigh of relief. She ought to get more involved in Brianna's school, but part of her remained reluctant to get sucked into the world of soccer moms, bake sales, and prom night.

She settled into her car and pulled out of the parking space to head to work. Or maybe she should go talk to one of the mothers present at the haunted house. A glance at her dashboard clock told her she still had time before her first client arrived. It couldn't hurt to pay a visit to Ricky's mom, for example. Hannah had been friendly to her at the event.

Marla pulled over to the curb and looked up the woman's address on the parent volunteer roster. She didn't live that far away. It would be worth a stop to see if the other parent was home.

Hannah answered the doorbell on the first ring.

"I'm sorry to disturb you," Marla said with a bright smile. "I was in the neighborhood and decided to stop by to see if you were okay. Brie and I are still upset by what happened."

"How thoughtful of you. Please come inside. I'm in the middle of making a vegetable stew for dinner." She eyed Marla's skirt and sweater ensemble. "You look nice. Surely you didn't dress up just for me?"

"No, I've been to the school, and now I'm on my way to work. I won't keep you long."

Hannah led her into the kitchen, where she picked up a

wooden spoon and stirred the ingredients in a Dutch oven on the stovetop.

"That smells great. What's in it?" Marla asked, watching steam rise from the simmering vegetables.

"Eggplant, onions, zucchini, tomatoes, and chickpeas. It's easy to make." Hannah put the spoon aside and replaced the glass cover. "So is checking on me the only reason you're here?"

"I'm wondering who will take over Mr. Ripari's class. Will they assign a substitute teacher or someone else?"

"Didn't you ask when you were there?"

"No, I was more concerned with security. Maybe they should hire a guard."

Hannah propped her hands on her hips. "Whatever for? They already have cameras everywhere."

Maybe so, but apparently not in the locker rooms. "I don't mean to scare you, but consider the people at the house last night. Mr. Ripari's murderer could be one of them."

"You're thinking a student or a parent we know might have killed the man? That's ridiculous. It has to be somebody who'd been hiding in the woods."

"For what purpose? Was he waiting for Mr. Ripari in particular to come outside? Or was the teacher merely a random victim? If that were true, more of us would have gotten the axe." A mental image of the box of fake weapons came to mind. What if they hadn't all been props?

"I don't know why you aren't letting the police do their job, dear. Isn't your husband a detective?"

"Yes, but the crime took place in another district. It wouldn't be his case, except for our daughter's involvement. Her world has been disrupted by this loss. How is your son doing?"

Hannah shot her a narrowed glance. "He's upset, even though he didn't like the man."

"Why is that?"

"Ricky wasn't doing well in his class."

"Oh, really? Perhaps a new teacher might be more lenient."

"What are you implying?" Hannah said in a tight voice.

"Nothing that matters at the moment. Tell me, have you met a student named Patrick Evans? I understand he got skittish whenever Mr. Ripari came around."

"We've met, but I barely know the kid. I believe Mr. Ripari was tutoring him."

"Didn't Mr. Ripari tutor your son? It might have helped raise his grade in history class."

"No way. I wouldn't want them alone in a room together."

"Why is that?" Marla wondered why Patrick might be uncomfortable around the man.

Hannah picked up a dishtowel to dry some dishes in the drainer. "I'd rather not say. I respected Mr. Ripari. He had a deep fondness for the region's history."

"Did that extend to his own family? Like, did he dig into his family roots to see if the claim against his property had any validity?"

"How would I know, Marla? And I don't care. The poor man is gone."

"The school receptionist told me he left his estate to the school in his will. Is that true?"

"This is the first I've heard of it. That would be most generous of him. The school needs renovations but hasn't had the funding."

"Yes, I could see the need for it when I was there. It's too bad Mr. Ripari never married and had a family of his own, though."

"You should ask Vicki Sweetwater. Rose's mother seemed to have some sort of hold on him. Her daughter got perfect grades in his class, and Ricky told me she wasn't any ace student."

"Wasn't Vicki there last night? I recall meeting her, but we didn't have a chance to chat."

"Yes, she's super protective and follows her child around like a mother hen. Vicki is the first parent to buy tickets whenever there's a school performance. Rose acts in the drama club," Hannah explained.

Marla watched as Hannah lifted the pot's lid, tossed in some freshly chopped parsley, and replaced the glass top. The aroma of sautéed onions made her mouth water. Aware she'd better grab lunch before going to work, she gestured toward the exit.

"I won't keep you any longer. I'm glad you and Ricky are okay. And thanks for taking me under your wing yesterday. It was my first volunteer effort as a parent, and I felt awkward."

"No problem." Hannah wiped her hands on the dishtowel and accompanied Marla to the front door. "It's a shame the haunted house got cancelled. The kids will have to come up with another fundraiser to subsidize their prom."

"How much money do they need?" Maybe Marla could do a charity event at the salon. She'd sponsored them before, where her stylists gave free cuts and blowouts and the money went to charity. It also brought in new customers, and so was a win-win either way. She mentioned her idea to the other woman.

Hannah smiled at the notion. "That would be wonderful, Marla. You're kind to offer."

"I'll look into it. I'm not sure how much of a dent our contribution would make, but it's an option. If it's doable, I'll let you know."

Chapter Four

On the way to her salon, Marla reconsidered her offer to hold a school fundraiser. It would be selfish of her to expect the other stylists to contribute their portion to Brianna's class. Usually, their charity events benefitted organizations like Locks of Love. She'd have to rethink her idea.

She parked at her shopping strip and detoured into Bagel Busters to speak to her friend, Arnie Hartman. His deli was a couple of doors down from the Cut 'N Dye Salon.

Arnie stood behind the cash register wearing his customary apron over a pair of jeans and a tee-shirt. His mustached face broke into a grin when he spotted her.

"Marla, my *shaineh maidel*. It's good to see you, pretty lady." He came around the counter to give her a quick embrace.

Marla stopped a passing waitress to put in her lunch order and then inquired about Arnie's wife and kids. The pleasantries out of the way, she spoke to him in a low tone.

"Guess what? A dead body turned up at one of Brie's school projects."

"Oy, vey. You're joking, right?" He noticed her serious expression. "Don't tell me you're the one who found it?"

"Yep, that's me." She gave him a quick rundown of events. Arnie had served as her sounding board on murder cases before, and he always made her feel better about things. Despite her cool, she did worry about Brianna at school until they unmasked the killer.

"You should keep a low profile," Arnie advised. "It's safer that way. It sounds as though you have a number of suspects, and you don't want the guilty party threatening Brianna because you're making waves."

"I know, but this case is eating at me. I can't help feeling our bad guy had to be present at the house. Dalton is looking into claims against the property. We'll see what he learns."

After catching up on more of Arnie's news, she collected her meal and headed to the salon. Work claimed her attention for the rest of the day. By the time she finally went home, ate a late dinner, and got ready for bed, it was ten o'clock.

She peeked in on Brianna to ask how her day had gone, but the teen was already asleep. Too tired to think straight, Marla postponed any discussion of events with Dalton until the next morning.

He brought up the subject on Friday at the breakfast table. "I haven't had time to check into the property claim against Mr. Ripari," he told Marla while unfolding the newspaper and separating its sections. "I have some other things to take care of today, and then hopefully I can do some research."

"That's okay. I'll be busy this weekend anyway. We're solidly booked at work." Marla stood at the sink and washed the frypan she'd used to make scrambled eggs. "Let's exchange news on Sunday when we're both off. I have to tell you what I learned yesterday at the school."

"What school?" Brianna bounded into the room, book bag in hand. Her dark brown hair swung in a braid down her back.

Marla gulped, confession time at hand. "I went to your high school yesterday to speak to the principal about school security."

"Why am I not surprised? I hope you won't become one of those helicopter moms."

"Your safety concerns me, and rightfully so. How did your day go?"

"Everybody was freaked out about Mr. Ripari's death. The school has counselors available."

"I hope you'll take advantage if you need to talk about it," Marla told her. "Your dad and I are here for you, too."

"Thanks, but I can take care of myself."

"I know, but I'll feel safer when the criminal is behind bars."

"I'm working my own angle, Marla. Stay away."

"What does that mean?" She put the pan into the dish drainer and dried her hands.

"I'm trying to get to know those kids better, the ones who helped us at the haunted house. Maybe I can learn something important."

Dalton rose, an ominous fold between his brows. "You keep your nose out of this, muffin. I'll handle it."

Marla staved off the rising tension by raising her hand in a stop signal. "Look, let's each do what we can, and we'll reconvene a council on Sunday to discuss our findings. Dalton, your daughter is in a good position to find out more about the students, as long as she's careful. I can tackle the parent angle. You look up the property's history. We'll get more done as a team."

Brianna smirked at her dad. "See, Marla appreciates me."

Dalton winced. "I hope we're not encouraging another amateur sleuth in the family. One of you is enough to give me gray hair."

"Your hair is already turning silver, Dad, and that change started years ago. This murder case isn't even assigned to your district, so you can't blame us for interfering. Any snooping on your part puts you in the same class."

Marla gave Brianna a packaged snack of fruit and nuts for her to add to her bag. "Speaking of classes, who's taking over for Mr. Ripari?"

"They've brought in a substitute. Mrs. Krizelman has taught our class before. I don't know if she'll stay for the next semester, though."

"So none of the other teachers are qualified to teach his classes?"

"It's possible, but their schedules might be full."

"That would eliminate professional competition as a motive." Marla, hearing the dogs bark, let them in from the fenced backyard and threw them each a biscuit.

Dalton grabbed his key ring from a hook by the garage door. "Come on, Brie. I'll give you a ride to the bus stop on my way out."

"Wait," Marla said, a sudden thought occurring to her. "Isn't there a football game tomorrow?"

"Yes, it's a home game." Brianna's face brightened as she caught the drift. "Oh, you think we should go and use the opportunity to question people."

"What time does it start? I'll have to juggle my appointments."

"I think it's an afternoon game. I can check and send you a text."

"Great. Dalton, can you clear your schedule to go?" Marla bent to scratch the poodle behind his ear when Spooks poked her ankle with his long snout.

"I'll make time. It would be a good chance to interview the people involved. Good idea, ladies."

Marla's pulse accelerated at the thought of attending a high school football game. It must have been eons since she'd gone to one. At least Brianna liked team sports. The girl could be bookish, but acting classes got her out of the house as did softball, when in season.

***

Saturday afternoon turned out to be a perfect day for a ball game. Marla wore a comfy short-sleeved top, jeans, and ankle boots. She'd bought the latter on her dude ranch honeymoon in Arizona and loved them. Actually, she'd loved everything about that trip to meet Dalton's extended family, except for the murders. Tromping through the dirt to the bleachers reminded her of the rodeo there.

"So I stopped by Hannah Westfield's house yesterday on my way to work," Marla announced, after Dalton had bought a trio of hot dogs and they'd taken seats to watch the game in progress. "She said Vicki Sweetwater had some sort of influence over Bill Ripari. Her daughter, Rose, got good grades in his class. Rose belongs to the drama club. How come you haven't joined, Brie? You take acting classes. I'd think it would interest you."

Her eyes shielded behind designer sunglasses, Brianna tilted her head. "I don't want to act in school plays or do live theater. If I were serious, I'd sign with a casting agent and go to auditions for film or TV gigs. My real goal is to improve my public speaking, so I can apply for the debate team next year."

"Really?" Dalton raised his eyebrows. "I had no idea. You'll be great."

Marla had no doubts about that statement. Brianna knew how to win an argument.

She wiped a smear of mustard off her mouth. Eating a hot dog at a sports game was the best part of being there. "So this Rose, do you know her well?" she asked the teen.

Brianna shrugged her slim shoulders. "Rose hangs out with Shaun from the football team. We don't run in the same crowd."

"Aren't you in history class with her?"

"No, she must have it another period. How does she interest you?"

"I'm wondering why Hannah said Rose's mother is overprotective."

"That's not unusual. Most moms are protective of their daughters."

"Yes, but I have a feeling something else is going on

here. Anyway, listen to this." Marla peered around to make sure nobody else was taking an interest in their conversation. "When I walked by the boys' locker room, I overheard a conversation between two kids. One of them mentioned pills the coach was giving him."

"What kind of pills?" Dalton demanded. A gust of wind tossed his hair, giving him an endearingly tousled look.

Marla ignored the sudden rush of heat that swept from her toes on up. She fixed her gaze on his molten steel eyes. "I don't know, but the boy isn't well. He's afraid to tell the coach for fear he'll be kicked off the team. Maybe it's vitamins, and I'm being an alarmist."

"Or not. I wonder if that kid was in Ripari's class."

"Why would it matter?"

"If the history teacher noticed the boy was ill and suspected the coach's involvement, it could provide a motive."

Brianna, finished with her hot dog, crumpled her napkin and stood. "I can find out. My friends are over there."

Marla followed the direction of her glance and noted Andy's tall frame and his head of sandy hair. Surrounded by a couple of other guys, he was looking their way.

Uh-oh. Trouble is brewing in teenage land. Marla hadn't given a second thought to what Brianna had worn to the game, but now she observed the girl's tight jeans and even tighter knit top. Good God, when had she started filling out like that? Marla shot her husband a glance, but thankfully he appeared oblivious.

"Go on." Marla shooed Brianna toward her friends, wondering if it was time for *that* talk with the girl. This was a wrinkle of motherhood she hadn't anticipated. To distract Dalton, she turned to him and babbled on regarding the school visit she'd made.

A gaggle of girls nearby shrieked at a move on the football field. Marla, lacking any comprehension of the game play, blocked them out. The sun warmed her shoulders, energizing her after the stress from the past couple of days.

"So let's count the suspects," Dalton said, ticking off each one on his fingers. "As far as teachers go, there's Coach Garsen. He was present the night of the murder and might have a motive, if what I'm thinking is true."

"Don't forget Principal Underwood. He might not have been at the house, but he could have paid someone to do the dirty deed. The school is a contender for Mr. Ripari's estate. Who's the executor, do you know?"

"The crime just happened on Wednesday, Marla. I've been busy doing other things, since technically this isn't my case. But I did dig deeper into the house's history. It's quite interesting. A man named Frank Conroy bought a large amount of agricultural land in western Broward in the 1930s. But after a particularly long drought one year, he sold most of his holdings."

"The janitor said Mr. Ripari's uncle might have secretly married one of the Conroy girls, and this means his estate should go to them."

"Let me continue. One of Conroy's biggest buyers was William Ripari, Senior, who built a large homestead on his two-hundred-acre purchase. Conroy blamed Ripari for greasing the hands of water management and diverting canals from being built so far out west. His lands might have prospered otherwise. Instead, he had to sell them at a reduced price."

"So that might account for bad blood between the families." Marla sat back as a couple of adults jostled down their row, arms laden with popcorn buckets and soft drinks. The smell of popped kernels made her hungry again. Or maybe being outdoors in the sun and fresh air stimulated her appetite. She watched the game with strapping young men running on the field while referees blew whistles. A horn sounded as the scoreboard changed.

"I'm not done," Dalton said with a note of impatience. "Eventually, Ripari Senior leased his territory to entrepreneurs for a pioneer theme park, with the caveat that his house be preserved. The park closed in 1964. At that time, his son Joseph Ripari tore down the tourist attractions and converted the original house into a restaurant. This lasted until he died and the restaurant closed."

Marla drew her own conclusions. "So our Mr. Ripari inherited the place but did nothing in the way of renovations. Didn't he have any siblings?"

"He was an only child, and the bloodline ended with him. He had an aunt, but she died childless. His uncle was killed in Vietnam."

"So how did those rumors about a marriage get started?"

"Conroy's daughter Janet was seen in the company of Ripari Senior's son, Nathan. The kid was drafted to Vietnam and didn't make it back."

"And people think Janet and Nathan might have secretly gotten married before he went overseas?"

"It wouldn't be the first time a hasty wedding took place during wartime."

"Okay, even if this union could be validated, how would it make the Conroys heirs to the estate?"

"I did find a record for the original William Ripari's will. It states that his property should pass to all married children equally, and from them to their descendants. Your history teacher was the sole living heir."

Marla bit her lower lip, ignoring the shrieks and chatter around them. "Neither his aunt nor his uncle had married, as far as anyone knew. If Janet had gotten pregnant—"

"Her child could claim the estate, assuming he had proof of his legitimacy."

"But you found no record of Janet's marriage to Nathan? The license would have been recorded somewhere."

"Maybe they married out of town. Remember, she'd have

been afraid of her father's reaction. He could have forced an annulment if he found out."

"Then Nathan must have kept a copy for safekeeping. His belongings would have been stored at the house, if that's where he'd been living before he shipped out."

Their eyes met. If any proof existed, it might lie among the dusty bric-a-brac in the history teacher's neglected estate.

Marla fell silent, watching the game and the glee of the observers. Her glance slid toward Brianna, who'd taken a seat next to Andy. Good, the teen wasn't engaged in interrogating her fellow students. This case had become more complex. The more she learned, the more confused she got as to who might have killed the poor history teacher.

"Oh, there's one of the moms," she said, waving her hand excitedly at the woman. "I'm going to run over for a chat."

Dalton gazed at her askance. "You're leaving me here alone?"

"You'll manage. You did okay before I came along." He must have attended school functions on his own between the time when his first wife died and when he met Marla. A single dad like him would have attracted female attention. After giving him a proprietary pat on the shoulder, she advanced down the bleacher row, careful to avoid people's feet.

Marla chatted briefly with the other mother before asking if the woman knew Vicki Sweetwater. "I understand her daughter is in the drama club. Mine is interested in joining."

"You're in luck, Marla. Vicki is here today. Everybody comes out for the home games."

Marla's cheeks heated. She should have come before this, but she'd avoided getting further involved in parental functions. It was time to own up to her responsibilities in that regard.

Pointed in Vicki's direction by her friend, Marla headed that way. Vicki wasn't hard to identify. She had straight black hair, heavily-lined cocoa brown eyes, and an outfit that showed her trying too hard to fit in with the younger generation. Creases framed her eyes as she smiled at Marla in friendly greeting.

"Marla, isn't it? We spoke briefly at the haunted house. I'm sorry we didn't have more time to talk that night before things went south. Rose has mentioned you since then."

"Has she? In a good way, I hope."

"She said you're a hairdresser and Brianna's stepmom. It was nice of you to volunteer. Bill's house would have been perfect for our school project."

Bill, and not Mr. Ripari. How well acquainted were the two of them? "Was Rose in his class?" Marla asked.

"Yes. My poor baby is still upset over his death, same as the other kids."

From the happy cries and screeching in the bleachers, Marla wondered if they'd already forgotten the sad event. "Do you know anyone who might have wanted to harm him?"

"Huh, get in line. Bill had more secrets than you have hair follicles, darling."

"Why do you say that?"

"I should know. We went to the same college."

Marla, standing on the sidelines with the other woman, gestured to an empty space on the nearest bleacher. "Let's sit a minute," she suggested. They'd be less conspicuous that way in the crowd. When Vicki didn't budge, Marla continued on, determined to get some answers. "Did you and Mr. Ripari keep in touch after graduation?"

"No, we lost track of each other."

"So how did you and Rose end up here?"

"Why do you care, Marla?"

"I found his body, and I'm married to a homicide detective. I've helped Dalton solve cases before. It's sort of what I do when I'm not at the salon."

Vicki shaded her face against the sun. "I heard you were

an unconventional mom. You shouldn't take risks that could hurt Brianna."

"She'd like to see Mr. Ripari's murderer put away as much as I would. I'd feel a lot safer about her going to school if I knew the killer was behind bars."

"If you're looking for leads, talk to Patrick Evans. Bill had been tutoring him."

"How come the man wasn't helping Ricky? From what I've understood, Hannah's son needed to improve his grades in history class."

"Hannah wouldn't let Bill be alone with her kid."

"Why not?"

Vicki leaned inward after casting a furtive glance around them. The only adult nearby was Mr. Lynch. The maintenance man was busy picking stray pieces of popcorn off the floorboards with a long tool and putting the debris into a bucket.

"Bill had different tastes. If I'd known then what I know now, I wouldn't have …."

"You wouldn't have what?" Marla prompted, when the woman failed to finish her sentence.

"I wouldn't have started things. It was a mistake I've paid for ever since." She glanced at Rose with a tender expression. "Well, not in every way."

Chapter Five

Did Vicki mean what Marla thought she meant? She supposed Vicki Sweetwater and Bill Ripari could have been in the same class.

"What did you study in college?" Marla asked in a casual tone, hoping to learn more about the woman's earlier relationship with the history teacher.

Vicki squared her shoulders. "I'm an accountant. I do mostly corporate work. Our busy season starts in another couple of months."

"I can imagine. Are you from Florida originally? Did you go to school here?"

"I went to University of North Carolina at Chapel Hill. Those were carefree days, at least until my last year." Her tone turned bitter. "I couldn't have known why he'd lost interest, could I? I'll bet he didn't even realize it himself. He did try to do the right thing, at least from his viewpoint, but I couldn't carry out his plan."

"Do you mean Mr. Ripari? Were you and he an item in college?"

"Whatever gave you that idea?" Vicki said with a false giggle, her eyes lacking mirth. "I'm talking about an old boyfriend. We graduated, and that was the end of it." She pointed toward a student cheerleader. "You should be more concerned about Maya. She wasted her efforts on Bill."

"How so?" Marla's forehead wrinkled in confusion at the change in subject.

"She tried to get Bill's attention in *that way*, but he wasn't interested. Maya should have let it go, but she could be spiteful when rebuffed."

Marla gaped at the teen performing with her group on the football field. "She meant to seduce Mr. Ripari? How did you hear about it?"

"Darling, I made it my business to learn everything about him. And her pathetic play for the man was rather obvious. Never mind that he could get dismissed for consorting with a student. That hasn't stopped him before, but usually he's more discreet. In this case, she wasn't his type. It took her a while to understand."

Marla shook her head. "I'm sorry, I don't follow how this relates to you."

"Never mind. What matters now is up to my lawyer."

"Can you be more explicit?"

"Let's talk about something more pleasant. I understand you own a beauty salon?"

Aware the woman wished to divert her attention, Marla chatted about her work, concluding their conversation by handing over a business card. Vicki didn't reciprocate.

Marla hurried back to Dalton, who'd acquired a bag of chocolate candies in her absence and was happily consuming them.

"You can check into their backgrounds to confirm they were a couple. Look for photos in their class yearbook," Marla finished in telling him her tale. "I'm wondering if Rose fits the timeline when they were together."

"You think she's Ripari's child?"

"It makes sense. Vicki had a bitter edge to her tone. Maybe she moved here to present Rose to him. It's possible he'd had no idea Vicki had gotten pregnant, especially if they graduated and lost track of each other."

"That's assuming Vicki had her own reasons for not confronting him sooner. Why now?"

"Maybe she married another man in the interim. She could be single again. Or she wanted to stake a claim on Rose's behalf for his estate, seeing as how he had no other heirs."

Dalton scrunched the empty candy wrapper in his hand. "You don't think she was involved in the murder, do you?"

"I wouldn't discount her. Both she and Rose were at the haunted house that night."

"Okay, so where do we go from here?"

Marla warmed under his affectionate perusal. She appreciated how he sought her opinions so readily now. "Vicki mentioned Patrick, a student whom Mr. Ripari was tutoring. She's the second person who's suggested I talk to the guy. He hangs out at a diner after school on weekdays. I'll go on Monday, and I can ask about Maya when I'm there."

"If the teacher rejected that girl, she'd have reason to resent him."

"We'll add her to the list. It would help if you touched base with the lead investigator to see if he'll share his progress."

"I'll give him a call during the week," Dalton said. "He can probably use some of the info we've gathered, plus he might have insights into these people's backgrounds."

By the end of the day, they each had their assignments. Brie would see what she could learn from the other students at school. Marla would join her after classes on Monday at the local hangout. And Dalton would continue his research into town records regarding the Conroy family. He'd also speak to the detective in charge of Ripari's case.

They stopped for dinner at a favorite restaurant before driving home. As Dalton turned into the driveway, he pointed to the front door.

"What's that on our stoop?"

"Where?" Marla peered out the window, but the sky had darkened, and she couldn't see too clearly. They hadn't expected to be home so late.

"I can't tell from here. Maybe it's a package. Are either of you expecting a delivery?"

"Not me," Brianna piped in from the back seat.

Curious to see what he'd spotted, Marla walked over as soon as he'd parked. She stopped under the porch light and sucked in a sharp breath.

A salon head lay face-up on the tile. Marla recognized the mannequin head as the same kind she bought for work. She used them to try new hair colors and styles.

This one's brunette hair and brown eyes looked eerily similar to hers, except this model had a knife stuck in its right eye.

She put a hand to her throat. "Dalton, you'd better come and see this," she hollered.

The dogs barked from inside the house as she felt time slowing. Fixated by the object, she couldn't move. Who would do this to them? The sender must have come by their place while they were at dinner.

"Good God," Dalton said upon noting the item.

Brianna skidded to a halt beside him. "Ugh, what is that thing?"

"It's the same type of head I experiment on in my salon. Do you think the person's prints might be on that knife handle?" Marla asked in a detached voice, as though this were happening to someone else. "I recognize its reddish tint. It looks like the same knife that killed Mr. Ripari."

"Don't touch anything. I'll get my evidence kit." Dalton loped off toward the garage.

"Let the dogs out first," she called as her rational mind returned. "They've been inside all day."

While waiting for his return, Marla snapped photos of the macabre gift with her cell phone. Soon the dogs quieted, and a heavy silence fell. Brianna stood by, staring at the item. Her young face looked pale.

"Brie, why don't you go inside? Your father will deal with this."

"Who do you think left it for us? And where did they buy this thing? Don't you order the heads from your suppliers?"

"Yes, but anyone can get them at a beauty supply store. Or at the party store this time of year," Marla added. "They have various body parts for Halloween decorations."

"Maybe this is just a prank," Brianna said with a hopeful note.

"I doubt it. We've riled somebody. I haven't a clue who it might be, though. Watch your back at school, honey. This worries me."

When Dalton took charge, she gave a sigh of relief and headed inside to relax. Yet her body refused to cooperate. As she lay in bed later, her muscles remained taut and her heart beat too fast.

"Do you think it's someone we spoke to at the football game?" she asked Dalton beside her. He smelled like shampoo, his hair freshly washed. Its silver strands glinted in the lamp light.

He switched channels on the bedroom TV. "I don't see how that's possible given the time frame. This would have to be planned. How many local places are there where you can buy a salon head like the ones you work on?"

"Not many. I order mine online."

"We should visit the stores tomorrow, assuming they're open on Sunday. Maybe we can track the sale to a place around here."

"Will you tell Detective Hanson about this development?"

"Let's see what we discover first."

"I promised Brie we'd go to the Halloween store. The holiday is next weekend, and she doesn't have her costume yet."

He put down the remote, a frown of disapproval creasing his brow. "Isn't she too old to go out? I don't like the idea of her roaming the streets with this business going on."

"It's not for trick or treating. She's invited to a party, now that she doesn't have to work at the haunted house."

***

Sunday dawned bright and sunny with a balmy Florida breeze. Marla's family took advantage of the good weather, treating the dogs to a couple of hours at the dog park. Brunch followed after the pets got dropped off at home. Finally, they headed to the Halloween store.

While Brianna selected her costume, Marla and Dalton cruised the aisles searching for styling heads like the one left on their doorstep. Marla discovered plenty of skulls and monster masks, but nothing resembling a true-to-life mannequin.

She suggested they try beauty supply stores next. Normally, she ordered her human hair heads from an online source, but local places might carry them.

They hit the jackpot at a place in Davie that carried a variety of choices. Marla skipped over the Miss Michelle Afro Head and the Mr. Brad model, but she paused at the Miss Sophia Manikin Head that sold for seventy-five dollars. Her heart thumped in excitement. The brown hair parted off-center looked similar to the one she'd received as an unwelcome gift.

"Excuse me," she said to the blonde at the cash register. Marla held up the head in her hand. "Has anyone bought one of these recently?"

"Let's see, that's Miss Sophia, right?" The clerk accessed her computer files. "Nope, I don't see any sales for that particular model in the past month. Mr. Brad is more of a hit. He costs forty-five dollars. Would you like me to get him for you?"

Marla put the head on the counter. "No, thanks. What other stores in the area might carry this model?"

The clerk mentioned a couple of other places, plus a

superstore east on Federal Highway. "Did you want to buy this gal?" she asked Marla.

"Yes, I'll get her along with one of your tripod stands." It might be fun to put her heads on display at the salon. If nothing else, they'd be conversation starters.

Their research took them further afield and racked up a higher bill. Marla bought a Chantal head with light brown hair and a Sabrina model with blond hair. She itched to start work on them, already imagining the colors and styles she could try.

"Look at this one," Dalton said at the last place on their list. "It's a balding guy. Who would want to buy him?"

"Don't knock it. Danny looks a lot like our male clients." Marla indicated the well-stocked shelves. "I'm going to come here for my heads hereafter. They have a huge selection."

"The brunettes all look the same to me," Dalton remarked in a bemused tone.

"On the contrary, their shades vary. Look, here's another Sophia head."

Unfortunately, her ploy to bribe the cashier for information didn't get too far. Neither did Dalton flashing his badge. The only bonus was learning that a Sophia head had been purchased within the past week.

"I'll get a warrant," Dalton told her in an undertone. "Then we can access the surveillance video as well. Our bad guy made a mistake in leaving that gift for you."

"Marla, can I get these items?" Brianna asked, dumping a pile of goods on the counter. She'd been busy shopping while they studied the mannequin heads.

"Sure, I'll take care of it." Marla took out her credit card and paid for the nail polishes, eye makeup, and ponytail holders that Brianna had selected.

"You shouldn't wear too much eyeliner," Dalton admonished his daughter. "It'll make you look easy."

"Really, Dad? I'm grown up now. Get over it."

Marla hoped Brianna would have no further concerns

than her appearance, grades, and social life. But in view of the history teacher's murder, she headed to Dee's Diner after school on Monday to chat with some of the students.

The restaurant was located in a busy shopping strip a few blocks away. From the number of cars parked in the lot, the diner looked to be popular among residents. Marla entered its brightly lit interior along with Brianna, whom she'd picked up from school before heading over there.

"How come you never told me about this place before? It's so quaint," she said.

They stood inside the entrance, where Marla gawked at the decor. Decorated in fifties style, the diner had cushioned booth seating and a counter section, plus a few separate tables for large groups. Waitresses wore frilly white aprons over black dresses with pearl jewelry. From their low-cut bodices and short hems, Marla could see why school boys might hang out here.

She recognized some of the faces among a group of youths, but no way could she barge in there as a lone adult. What was the best way to make her approach?

Brianna tugged on her arm. "Come on. I know these kids."

From the girl's terse voice, Marla surmised this was difficult for her as well. She dutifully followed along, drawing over a chair in imitation of the teen's action.

"Hey, guys. This is my stepmom, Marla. She's absolutely starving, so I thought we'd stop by here. What's good to eat?"

"I like the burgers and milkshakes," said one girl. While Brianna engaged her in conversation, Marla waved to Jules, whom she remembered from the haunted house. He had the complexion of a ghost, as though he hibernated indoors during the school year.

"Hi, I remember you from Mr. Ripari's house," she called to him. "That was a terrible night."

"Rest in peace, Mr. R-I-P Ripari," sneered a youth at his side. This kid had a snub nose, a broad forehead, and a head of thick black hair. He regarded Marla with an unfriendly stare.

"I'm sorry, we haven't met," she said to him.

Jules responded. "This is my friend, Patrick." He nudged the guy. "Mrs. Vail is married to a cop. Brie's dad is a police detective."

Did Marla detect a note of warning in his tone? "That's right. I've heard Mr. Ripari was tutoring you in history, Patrick. I know Ricky had some trouble in his class and was wondering why he didn't get help after hours."

"Ricky wouldn't put up with his shit."

Marla, taken aback by the vehemence in Patrick's tone, couldn't immediately think of a comeback. "Didn't Mr. Ripari help you as a tutor?" she asked after a moment.

"He helped himself more than he did me."

Jules poked him again. "Patrick, be careful what you say. The man is gone. He can't hurt anybody now."

Marla pounced on his words. "The teacher hurt you? In what way?"

Patrick shot her a hooded glance. "What's it to you?"

"I'm a concerned parent, especially if a student is harmed."

"Well, don't be. Like the dumb principal would do anything in this case. He wants Mr. Ripari's property too badly. Principal Underwood would brag about how they were friends and how the history teacher's will favored the school." He snickered. "I know what kind of *friends* they were."

Oh, my. Marla got an inkling of what he meant, and it made sense on many levels. But how could she get one of these people to come out and say it?

"Hey, here comes the deadly duo," Jules proclaimed. His fingers drummed on the table, adding to his jerky motions. The guy couldn't seem to sit still. His gaze darted about the room like a hunted rabbit.

Haunted Hair Nights

Marla raised her head as a pair of girls arrived, ogling the fellows. Brianna came to her rescue, introducing Maya and Rose. The former barely covered her skin in a skimpy outfit and oozed sex appeal in the way she moved, while Rose dressed more demurely. Rose kissed a buff fellow on the lips. Oh, yes. Wasn't that Shaun from the football team?

"Hi, Rose. Good to see you again. We met at the haunted house."

The girl gave a nervous glance at the others. "Oh, right. How are you, Mrs. Vail?"

"I'm good, thanks." The waitress interrupted, and Marla placed her order for a bowl of mushroom barley soup. She sat back to listen as the teens engaged in school chitchat. Brianna held her own with this bunch, but it clearly wasn't her normal crowd. She kept glancing at the entrance as though wishing she were elsewhere.

Feeling like an outsider as well, Marla had a sudden revelation that took her breath away. Aside from Brianna, didn't all of these kids have a reason to resent Mr. Ripari?

Chapter Six

"I think they all might be guilty," Marla said to Nicole at work on Tuesday, after bringing her colleague up to date.

"Get out of town. You can't believe a bunch of kids conspired to commit murder," Nicole replied. The cinnamon-skinned stylist looked as sleek as ever in a patterned maxi-dress, her black hair clipped atop her head and her face expertly made-up. Nicole loved to read mystery novels, so Marla could always count on her to debate suspects in a logical manner.

She'd brought to work the mannequin heads and tripod stand she had purchased the day before. Hopefully, she would have a chance to work on them today. Although her schedule was full for the first few hours, maybe later she'd have some spare time.

The aroma of brewing coffee drifted her way from the coffee pot set up for customers. Robyn, the receptionist, had gone to Bagel Busters for their morning order. Everything sparkled from a fresh cleaning the night before.

Marla lined up her favorite products and plugged in her tools in preparation for the day. "The bad guy has to be a teacher, parent, or student. On the teacher side, there's Principal Underwood. He's hoping to gain from Mr. Ripari's death by the provisions in his will. Underwood must mean to impress the school board. Having a generous benefactor for his facility can only be to his advantage."

Nicole frowned at her. "I thought you said another family had filed a claim for the estate."

"That would be the Conroys. Dalton is researching that aspect." Marla stowed her handbag in a drawer and then stared at Nicole. "You've reminded me of something. The missing marriage certificate would prove their inheritance rights. It could be hidden inside the house in the woods. Mr. Ripari never lived there. After the restaurant closed, the place was shuttered."

"Wait, tell me the history again. I forgot the details."

"Frank Conroy bought the land in the 1930s for agricultural use. After a drought, he sold his holdings at a steep discount to William Ripari, Senior. Ripari built a house on the estate. Years later, he leased the property to a consortium for a pioneer theme park, with the caveat that his house be preserved as a historical exhibit."

"So he moved out at the time?"

"Obviously. Anyway, when the tourist park closed, his son Joseph tore down the attractions but kept the house. He converted it into a successful restaurant. This establishment lasted until he died."

Nicole leaned against her counter. "So what happened then?"

"Joseph's heir—our deceased history teacher—restored the home's furnishings that had been left in storage, but he never moved in. I'd guess his appreciation of history made him hang onto the place, until he received an offer to buy the property. The buyer's proposal promised to save the residence as part of a living history attraction."

"That sounds like a good compromise. How does the Conroy family fit in?"

"Frank Conroy blamed Ripari Senior for the devaluation of his land. Frank had a daughter. Rumor says Janet had a secret relationship with Ripari's other son, Nathan."

"They would have had to meet in secret if their fathers disapproved."

"It's a Romeo and Juliet thing, right? Nathan would have been our Bill Ripari's uncle, but he was drafted to Vietnam and didn't make it back."

"And you think it's Nathan who hid the marriage certificate in his family's house?"

Marla tapped her chin in thought. "He must have believed it was the safest place at the time. If Janet kept the document, her father might have found it and annulled their marriage."

"So it would be Janet who is filing a claim on the property?"

"We don't know if she's still living. She'd have to be in her seventies. It's possible she was pregnant when Nathan left to go overseas."

"So it could be her child who learned about their family history and wants a piece of the pie?"

"Exactly. And the proof might be hidden in the house."

"You don't want to go back there, Marla." The front door bells chimed, and Nicole jerked her head up. It was Robyn returning with their bagels and cream cheese. "You were telling me about the teachers who might be involved. Besides the principal, is there anyone else?"

"Yes, one of the gym instructors who also happens to be the football coach. I overheard a student mention pills the coach gave him."

"Like he'd hurt himself, and the man gave him an Advil? What's the harm in that?"

"No, this kid was feeling ill, and another student cautioned him against taking the pills the coach gave out. His team members all look rather beefy."

"You're thinking steroids, or something worse? Could he be dealing to the kids?"

"It's possible. Now that I remember, I saw the janitor rummaging around in the boys' gym lockers the other day. Maybe he suspects something, too. That man seems to have eyes everywhere." Marla glanced out the front window. "Here comes my first customer. We'll have to continue this talk later."

They got back on track at lunchtime, when both were munching sandwiches and drinking coffee in the back storeroom. It was after two o'clock, but they'd been too busy with clients beforehand. Without preamble, Marla launched into her suspicions regarding Brianna's fellow students.

"I count at least five of them. And most were present that night at the haunted house. Jules Jamison is a nerdy student who acts like he's wired on something. He's friends with Patrick Evans, who was being tutored by Mr. Ripari. Except, I'm not certain that's all the history teacher was doing with him. I get vibes that tell me it was a troubled relationship."

"Meaning what?" Nicole, soaking in Marla's litany with wide eyes, sat on a stool. She took a bite of her ham and cheese sandwich.

"I think the history teacher made a pass at Patrick. That would account for Maya's resentment. She's the type who gets what she wants through sex. She must have tried to have her way with Bill Ripari and got rebuffed."

"I see where you're going with this. Who else is in the group?"

"Ricky Westfield was failing history class. Neither he nor his overprotective mother would want that to happen. Vicki Sweetwater is the same way about her daughter, Rose. She knew Bill in college, and I got the impression they had an intimate relationship. Rose might be the man's daughter, in which case she could claim inheritance rights. Rose dates Shaun, who's on the football team. And we already know something odd is going on between the coach and his players. That's the bunch of them."

"Wow, this case is a tough one. What about clues?"

Marla chewed a morsel of her turkey sandwich and swallowed. "The knife that killed Mr. Ripari is a similar type to the one left in a mannequin head at my doorstep."

Nicole sat up straight. "What? You didn't mention this before."

Marla filled her in. "We've found a local place where the person might have bought the head. Dalton is trying to get a warrant so he can watch the surveillance video and obtain the sales records."

"That would be helpful." Nicole, having finished her meal, stood and tossed the empty wrapper in the trash. "There's another thing you haven't mentioned, and that's people's alibis. Has Dalton mapped out everyone's locations for that night?"

"Good point, I'll ask him." Her cell phone rang. Marla dug it out of her pocket. "It's Brie. She should be in class now. I wonder what she wants. Hello, what's up, hon?"

"Can you come and get me at school?" Brianna asked in a tremulous tone.

"Sure, what's wrong?" Her heart fluttered with alarm. Something upsetting must have happened.

"I'll tell you when you're here. I'll be waiting in the front office. Hurry, Marla."

***

Marla made it to the school in record time. She hustled into the administrative suite while tamping down the panic squeezing her chest.

The sight of Brianna's familiar face restored her equilibrium. She hugged the teen, then stepped back to inspect her. Nothing appeared amiss.

"What's this about, hon?" The aroma of potato chips reached her nose. Connie, the desk clerk, had an open bag by her station. She stared at them in blatant curiosity.

"Come with me, and I'll show you." Brianna marched her to a series of lockers and swung one open. "I found this inside today between afternoon periods."

Marla gasped as she viewed another mannequin head, similar to the one left on their doorstep at home. This lady had brown hair in a ponytail and dark brown eyes like Brianna. Again, a knife was stuck into an eye.

"Dear Lord. I can see why you'd want to go home," she told the teen, putting an arm around the girl's slim shoulder.

"I don't feel safe here, Marla. I just want to leave."

"Did you call your dad? He'll want to dust your locker for prints and bag the evidence."

"He wanted to drive straight over here, but I told him to send someone else. I'd call you to come and get me. I can't keep bothering Dad every time something bad happens."

"I understand, but he worries about you. And this incident warrants a police report."

A pained look came into Brianna's eyes. "I know, but I don't want to wait around for the cops."

"If we leave this head here, the person who put it inside your locker might remove it before the officer arrives," Marla mused. "We should bring it to your father."

Brianna pointed to Mr. Lynch mopping the hallway. "The janitor might be able to get us a brown bag. I'll ask him." The teen hurried away before Marla could protest.

Was it her imagination, or did that man always seem to be around when something happened? She watched as Brianna spoke to him. He gave her a curt nod before scurrying off.

While Brianna waited for their makeshift evidence bag, Marla took out her cell phone and snapped photos of the head from different angles. She took a few close-ups of the knife this time, since the lighting was better than it had been on her front stoop.

Once they'd bagged the head, she approached Mr. Lynch. "Hi, I'm wondering who has access to these lockers."

The lean man in a gray uniform smoothed a lock of black hair off his forehead. "The students put in their own combinations, miss. Is there a problem?"

"Yes, someone broke into my stepdaughter's locker and left something inside that gave her a fright. So I repeat. Who could have gained access to her space?"

His weasely blue eyes met her stern gaze. "I rightly dunno."

"Do you have a master combination so you can get in for emergencies, or if a student can't remember the code?"

"We keep a log of all the codes, miss. But I don't like what yer implying."

"I'm not accusing you of anything. Could somebody else have acquired these numbers?"

His brows lifted like twin airplane wings. "The principal has the combinations. Maybe someone copied it from his office, although I think he keeps the file on his computer."

"All right, I'll stop in there."

"What is it you found, miss, if I might ask?"

She opened the bag to show him and gauge his reaction. He made a choked sound.

"Good God Almighty. Who would leave such a thing for a young 'un?"

"That's what I'd like to find out." Marla tapped his suntanned arm. His skin had brown spots like many older Floridians, yet he couldn't be past his forties, could he? Had the man lived here all his life? "Tell me, the night Mr. Ripari died at the old house, did you go outside at all?"

"No, miss. I was busy cleaning away the cobwebs, the real ones. And that place was awfully dusty. I was happy to earn extra money getting it in shape."

"But you never got paid, did you? Wasn't it Mr. Ripari who'd hired you for the night?"

"That's correct, miss." His mouth compressed, but his eyes held a gleam of something other than dismay at the lack of a paycheck. "I was so upset by his death that I went right home."

"And where is that, Mr. Lynch?" He mentioned a trailer

park in Cooper City. "So you didn't go outdoors between the time I saw you inside the house and when I found the body? Did you happen to glance out a window and see anyone prowling the grounds?"

He shook his head. "I wish I had, because I can't think who'd want to harm the poor sap. I guess what they say is true. The son must pay for the sins of his forefathers."

The bible verse doesn't go like that. It's more like, fathers shall not be put to death because of their children; nor shall children be put to death because of their fathers. Each one shall pay for his own sin. But your meaning is clear. You know about the feud between the Conroys and the Riparis.

Marla would have liked to continue this conversation, but Brianna was gesturing for her to move along. She thanked the janitor for his assistance and turned away.

One more stop was on her agenda. She wouldn't leave without a visit to the principal's office to show Mr. Underwood the item in the bag and to mention how Brianna's locker was breached.

The principal's eyes bulged as he regarded the knife stuck in the mannequin's face. "How did that weapon get into this school? Connie! We have a situation." He stalked into the outer office and confronted the receptionist. "Get me our security officer. He isn't doing his job."

"Excuse me?" Marla said, following at his heels. Brianna was seated in the reception area out by Connie's station. "This is what bothers you? My daughter's locker was broken into and this item placed in there. Shouldn't you be more concerned about her well-being?"

Principal Underwood glowered at her. "Weapons are not allowed on our premises. I'll take that, please." He extended his hand to grab the bag, but Marla snatched it away.

"I should say not. This is going to the police." Her body stiff, she regarded him with her most imperious glare. "My husband is sending an officer to investigate. If you cooperate,

I won't leak the incident to the press. We wouldn't want other mothers to panic."

She signaled to Brianna. "Come on, let's go. Oh, and Brianna will be out sick for a few days. Consider this my notice."

Once they passed through the exit, Marla shook her head in disgust. "I can't believe that man didn't care about your reaction. He's more concerned about his school's public image."

Yes, said her inner voice, *and how far would he go to boost his own interests there?*

"They have cameras in the hallways," Brianna mentioned as they walked to Marla's white Camry. "Maybe Dad can get a copy of the video."

"Good idea." Marla unlocked the car doors as they approached. "I wonder if he got a warrant for the beauty supply store. This head might have come from the same place."

Brianna slid into her seat and gave Marla a contrite glance. "I'm sorry I called you at work. We can go to the salon. I know you'll have appointments to finish."

Marla thought a moment. She didn't want to leave Brianna home alone, even with the dogs present. The salon was a better option until she finished for the day, and the company might cheer the girl and put color back in her cheeks. But they had another stop to make first.

At the police station, Dalton moved from behind his desk to embrace his daughter. "Brianna, are you all right?" he asked, concern lacing his voice.

"I'm scared. Somebody got into my locker."

"I know. Tell me again what happened."

After they took seats and the girl related her tale, Marla handed over the paper bag. "We didn't want to leave the head there in case the same person came by to retrieve it."

Dalton peeked inside and muttered an expletive. "You took evidence from the scene?"

"I know we shouldn't have touched anything, but Brie wanted to leave. I didn't trust this to still be there by the time your officer arrived."

"That was the wrong move, Marla." His jaw clenched as he regarded her with a stern expression.

"I'm sorry, but maybe you can get some prints off it, and I have photos." She reviewed what they'd learned so far and whom she'd spoken to at the school. Her tale seemed to calm him. His shoulders relaxed, and the lines of tension eased on his face. "Have you made any progress?" she asked in conclusion.

He gave a solemn nod. "Detective Hanson has identified the murder weapon. It bears the same distinctive rosewood handle and brass trim as this one and the package left on our doorstep. The cocobolo knife runs about a hundred dollars and is available online from major suppliers of camping and hunting equipment."

"You mean, anybody can buy it? Do the local stores carry this model?"

"The sporting goods places might have it. My point is that it's a common weapon."

"Common to people who like the outdoors." Marla shuddered. If this knife weren't associated with a man's death, she might have admired its polished wood handle, stainless steel blade, and shiny brass trim.

"What's cocobolo?" Brianna asked in a meek tone. She'd been sitting there silently while they spoke.

Dalton folded his hands on the desk. "According to my research, it's a tropical hardwood from Central America. Only the heartwood portion of the tree is used. That's where you get the reddish color. Since it holds up well to repeated handling and exposure to water, it's commonly used in gun grips and knife handles, like this model. Cocobolo wood is also used for custom-made items, such as cue sticks, luxury pens, jewelry boxes, and even musical instruments."

"It is a pretty color," Marla admitted. "Which one of our suspects might own something like this? Did you get any prints from the package left on our doorstep?"

"Yes, but there's no match in the system."

"That's too bad. How about the murder weapon?"

"Unfortunately, our killer was clever that night. Hanson's team didn't get any clear prints. Our scumbag messed up with these heads, however."

"At least that's something. I'd suggest you request the surveillance video from Brie's school along with the one from the beauty supply store."

"I'll work on it. Do you want me to drive you home?"

"No, we'll be all right. I thought we'd go back to the salon. Come on, Brie."

During the ride through the streets of Palm Haven, a question came to mind. "Do any of the students who were at the haunted house care for camping and fishing or that sort of thing?"

Brianna shrugged. "I have no idea. Before this happened, I didn't know any of them that well. I suppose most of the crowd will be at the Halloween party this weekend. How appropriate that it's Friday the Thirteenth."

"Where is it being held?" Marla should have known this already.

"Dee's Diner is throwing the bash. The owner says she wants to sponsor more events that school kids can safely attend."

"That's generous of her."

"Yes, it is. Since we're not doing the haunted house, this gives us somewhere to go. And Mr. Underwood said he might stop by." Brianna clasped her hands in her lap. "I'm not sure I want to go. The person who left me this head might be there."

"And that's exactly why we have to show up."

With all of the suspects present in one place, perhaps they could finally draw a bead on the killer.

Chapter Seven

The following day brought several developments. Dalton called Marla at work during the late afternoon on Wednesday to tell her Mr. Ripari's body had been released.

"It's about time," she said, gripping her cell phone close to her ear with one hand and wiping down her station with the other. In between clients, she had a few moments to chat.

"Will there be a memorial service?"

"Not to my knowledge. Get this. Vicki Sweetwater claimed the body and said she'd arrange for a burial. She showed a paternity test that proved Bill Ripari was her daughter's father."

"Vicki must have gotten pregnant her last year in college," Marla figured.

"She told Hanson that Bill knew about the baby. He paid her to get an abortion and believed she'd done so, but she had the child instead. They'd already graduated. Knowing he wanted nothing to do with the kid, she never told him the outcome. She married, and the other guy raised Rose as his own daughter. But when he died, Vicki felt compelled to learn what had happened to Bill. After she located him, they moved here, and Rose enrolled in his school."

"Did Rose know the history teacher was her real dad?"

"Yes, Vicki told her. She's contesting the will on her daughter's behalf."

"Do you think she told Mr. Ripari about Rose, and he rejected the girl? Maybe Vicki killed him out of resentment."

"Nuh-uh. I got my warrants earlier and watched the videos from the beauty store and the school. In both instances, the person handling the heads looked to be a guy. His features were hidden by a baseball cap and jacket, but it was definitely a male."

"That eliminates any mothers from the suspect list," Marla concluded. "How about the sales receipts for the mannequin heads?"

"They trace back to Coach Garsen, but he says his credit card was stolen last week. He'd reported it to his credit card company."

"Do you believe him?"

"Not necessarily. Detective Hanson learned he'd been fired from his previous position for giving steroids to the kids on his team. From what you've told me, I suspect he's doing the same thing here."

"How did he get the job at Brie's school with a record like that?"

"Principal Underwood owed him a favor. By the way, Underwood has a valid alibi for the night of Ripari's death."

"So that lets him off the hook but not the football coach. Maybe Mr. Ripari found out about Coach Garsen, and it got him killed."

"Perhaps, although I think Garsen would have been cleverer in planning a murder."

"Who's your prime suspect at this point?"

"I'd rather not say."

Marla didn't appreciate his clipped tone. "You know you can trust me. Why are you shutting me out?"

"I could still be wrong. As the noose tightens, the bad guy will get more desperate. We should make sure Brie isn't alone for the rest of the week."

"She doesn't want to go to the party on Friday night."

"Hanson will be there, and so will I. We're planning to close the net and nab the guy. Brie should attend. It would seem off if she wasn't there. Don't worry; I'll make sure she's safe."

"Okay, I'll convince her. What are you going to do, set a trap?"

"Exactly. It should be a Halloween to remember."

***

To set the mood on Halloween night, they all wore costumes. Brianna eschewed the latest movies for ideas and went with classic Belle from *Beauty and the Beast*. The booklover suited her nature, and so did Belle's view of the world. The ever-popular heroine looked past a person's appearance to gauge their true personality.

Marla and Dalton wore their western outfits from Arizona, embellished with fake spurs and neck scarves. Dalton's gun was authentic, although the sheriff's badge pinned to his fancy cowboy shirt was a Halloween store purchase. They'd bought boots while on their honeymoon out west, and Marla wore hers proudly. She had even learned to ride a horse at the dude ranch.

Sitting in the car with Dalton and Brianna on the way to Dee's Diner, she swallowed her nervousness. All of the principle players in Bill Ripari's murder would be present tonight. Would their plan work?

When they arrived, the restaurant was already crowded with revelers in all manner of disguises. Marla's heart sank as they approached the brightly lit place, the only storefront open that evening in the shopping strip. How would they be able to tell who was who?

The proprietor, dressed as a witch, had set out free fruit punch and appetizers and presented a special themed menu for anyone wanting to order a heavier meal. Kids stood in clusters, their parents socializing in another corner. Not too many adults remained, most having dropped off their teens for the duration of the party. Pumpkin spice scent from candles filled the air, while jack-o'-lanterns grinned from various corners. Orange and black streamers hung from the ceiling along with glittery ghost and goblin decorations.

Brianna set off on her job of chatting up her classmates to learn who was behind each outfit. Marla and Dalton moseyed over to the adults. She recognized Detective Hanson in the trench coat and Sherlock Holmes hat. Really? Could he have been more obvious? But then again, Dalton wasn't hiding his identity too well, either. What was it with lawmen?

With Brianna's help, Marla learned which students were the persons of interest in their case.

Jules stood by Patrick, the troubled kid whom Mr. Ripari had been tutoring. Jules seemed protective of the guy, which seemed a role reversal. With his pale complexion and scrawny limbs, Jules looked like he would need a champion in a fight. His hyperactive movements gave him away. He wore a skeleton outfit, appropriate to his thin frame. A fake firearm strapped to his back looked like it came from a *Ghostbusters* film.

Patrick hid behind a monster mask, his body enveloped in a brown robe. He kept scanning the crowd, as though fearful of who might approach him.

Maya Alvarez appeared to be making a play for the coach, from the look of her body language. The vamp seemed to prefer adults to seduce, perhaps so she could control them. Coach Garsen hovered by the refreshment table, keeping a watchful eye on his team and stuffing hors d'oeuvres into his mouth.

Rose Sweetwater had her arm hooked into Shaun's, the football player. They hung out with other team mates, including the kid Marla had overheard in the locker room. She recognized his scratchy voice as she idled on by.

After a suitable interval, she signaled Dalton across the room. Time for their little drama to begin. She cast a glance at

Brianna, who stood with a group of girlfriends by a side wall. Hmm, how come the boy she liked wasn't here? As Dalton had advised earlier, Brie had a clear path to the kitchen for a quick escape out a rear door, should their safety become compromised.

Dalton blew a police whistle. "Listen up, people. We have a real monster in our midst. We know who killed your history teacher, Bill Ripari."

Gasps sounded around the room, along with the noise of glass breaking. Patrick had dropped a glass of punch.

"Sorry," he said to the owner who rushed over. "I can't stand hearing that man's name."

"Who is it, Mr. Vail?" asked one of the mothers in a bold tone. Marla recognized her as Hannah in her cat costume. "And is this the appropriate place to announce your news? It's a student party. You two shouldn't even be here." Her gesture indicated both Marla and Dalton.

"Then why didn't you just drop off your kid, Mrs. Westfield? Is it because you know Ricky is guilty? We've discovered he hacked into the school computer system last week." Dalton nodded at the tall, gangly boy. "He altered his grade from a failing F to a passing B and stole the locker combination codes."

"Me?" Ricky pointed to his chest, encased in a white Storm Trooper uniform. "I wouldn't even know how to do that."

"Or was it your mom?" Dalton pointed to Hannah. "Did she gain access to Brianna's locker and leave her a mannequin head with a knife in its eye?"

Hannah's jaw dropped open. "How horrible. I did no such thing. How dare you accuse either one of us? I'll report you for harassment, officer."

"Your son must be responsible, then. Who else among this crowd has the smarts to hack into the school system?"

"Jules can do it," Ricky said, pointing to his friend. "He's always bragging about how he can get around any computer. Was it you? Did you change my grade?"

"Hey, don't complain," Jules said with a disdainful tilt of his nose. "I did you a favor, man. I hacked into Mr. Ripari's files and figured I'd fix a few things while I was there."

Ricky stared at him. "Why'd you do something so stupid? I didn't ask you to cheat on my behalf."

"I did it for Patrick's sake." Jules turned to the rest of them. "Mr. Ripari was supposed to be tutoring Patrick. Instead, the filthy old man made a move on him. I'd hoped to get evidence to leak to the press. This wasn't the first time he'd hit on a student. He couldn't be allowed to continue his abuse."

Patrick gazed at him in horror. "I would have gotten out of my own mess."

"No, you wouldn't, man. You were too afraid of disappointing your dad if you flunked history class. You let that jerk do those awful things to you so he'd give you an A."

"Be quiet, Jules." The boy's voice choked. "I didn't want anyone else to know. It's over now anyway."

"It's over because I ended it. Accessing his files didn't get me what I wanted, so I took other measures. And if Brianna and her stepmom hadn't gone snooping, things would have been fine. You didn't pay any attention to my warnings, did you?"

"So you're the one who left us those gifts?" Marla said in a disbelieving tone. She found it hard to fathom that this pasty-faced kid had the chutzpah to kill a man.

Jules sneered at them. "You're all cowards. You talk a lot, but you do nothing. I'm the only one with the guts to take action."

Dalton's shoulders hunched as he approached. "Did you think we wouldn't find out about your camping trips with your father? Is that where you gained a fondness for those rose-handled knives? We got some good prints off them, but there wasn't any match in the system. I'll bet they match yours."

"Those knives are my signature, man. But this can be, too." Jules yanked the weapon off his back and waved it at the crowd. "Now this here ain't no fake. I took it from my father's gun collection. He'll understand that I have to go away for a while. He'll be proud of me for standing up for what's right. Get out of my way."

"Easy, son." Dalton halted and spread his hands. "No one has to get hurt."

"You're damn right," Detective Hanson said. While Dalton had captured the kid's attention, Hanson had been edging closer from behind. Now he wrenched the weapon from Jules's grasp.

After a brief scuffle, Dalton cuffed Jules and shoved him over to Hanson.

"He's yours now. I don't envy you notifying his parents."

"I know. Hey, thanks for your help. I wasn't sure your strategy would work. I'd have brought the kid straight in for questioning."

Dalton gave Marla his special smile. "I've learned subtler methods sometimes work better."

Marla smiled back then sobered. "I'm sorry for Jules' family."

"So am I." Patrick's disconsolate expression tore her heartstrings. "He did it for me. I'd never have wanted the history teacher to die, despite his issues."

"People have done worse things out of loyalty," Marla said to comfort him. She scanned the crowd. "Aren't we missing somebody tonight? I thought Mr. Lynch had been hired to do the cleanup. Has anyone seen him around?"

Dalton poked her. "I'll bet I know where we can find him. Let's go. If we hurry, we might catch him in the act."

Chapter Eight

"How did you know where to look for Mr. Lynch?" Brianna asked her father during their Sunday morning stroll at the local nature preserve. "I'd never have guessed he would have gone to the house in the woods on Halloween."

"He knew everybody was occupied at the Halloween party," Dalton said, thumbs hooked on his belt. "It was the perfect opportunity for him to search for proof of his parents' marriage without fear of discovery."

Marla kept pace along the winding path through the wetlands. The smell of dank earth and decaying vegetation filled the warm autumn air. They needed a cold spell to bring temperatures down and make walking outdoors more comfortable.

"I can't believe he found it," she added. "Who would have thought to look inside the hollow arm of a white plaster statue?"

"It was clever of Nathan Ripari to hide it there," Dalton agreed. "Too bad he never got to tell Janet, his secret bride, where he'd put it. Back in his day, the property must have had lots of those statues around. Mr. Lynch was lucky this one hadn't been sold."

"Or broken apart by the elements," Brianna commented as they passed a mangrove section, where tree roots reached deep into the soggy soil. "So how did you determine Mr. Lynch was their son?"

Marla tilted her head to hear the reply. They hadn't had

Haunted Hair Nights

time to have this conversation earlier. Friday night, they'd been too tired after discovering Mr. Lynch at the historic house and exposing his identity. Then Saturday, Marla had a full day at work. Last evening, she and Dalton had a dinner date with Arnie and his wife. So today was the first time they could review the case.

"His age was about right," Dalton said, "and something about him bothered me. He'd told Marla he lived at a trailer park, but his address didn't check out."

"Principal Underwood hired him. You'd think he would have done a background check." Brianna sidestepped around a tree trunk in their path.

"Thomas Lynch revealed his true identity to the principal and promised to donate a portion of his inheritance to the school if he could prove his heritage. For Underwood, it was a win-win either way. If Lynch couldn't prove his parents' marriage, the school would still benefit upon Mr. Ripari's death. Meanwhile, Lynch kept close to Ripari, in case his cousin discovered the document's hiding place."

"How odd to think they were related," Marla said.

"Bill Ripari was Joseph's son, while Tom Lynch was Nathan's kid. Joseph and Nathan were brothers. Nathan wasn't aware Janet was pregnant when he was drafted into the army. She later married a man named Garvin Lynch."

"So the janitor hoped to prove his heritage and stake a claim on the estate?"

"Ripari Senior meant for the property to be equally divided among his married children or their heirs. That meant Nathan's son would be entitled to a share. Mr. Lynch knew Bill intended to sell the estate and wanted his half."

"Wasn't there a sister also?" Brianna asked with a confused frown.

"Yes, Joseph and Nathan had a sister, but she died childless." Dalton paused beside a tall tree enveloped by a strangler fig. "You know what gets me. The Conroy family wasn't left destitute after William Ripari bought their property. Frank bought a house on the New River, where he raised his two children. His son, Steven, became a lawyer and remained in the house after Frank died. Janet had remarried and lived elsewhere, but eventually the house passed to her. Steven was single and had no offspring."

Her mind reeling, Marla resumed their walk. "Wait, so you're saying the school janitor lives in a mansion on the New River? Those properties are worth millions."

"Now they are. They weren't worth much in Frank's day. It had gotten to the point where Tom Lynch was having trouble paying taxes. He figured if he could prove his mother's claim that she'd been married to a Ripari, he'd make enough money from the real estate deal Bill Ripari had mentioned, that he'd be comfortable into his old age."

"Now with Mr. Ripari dead and no heirs, does that mean he inherits everything?" Brianna asked, her sneakers making squishy noises as they passed a wet section.

Vines trailed down from overhead trees, with the possibility of spider webs lurking among them. Beams of sunlight penetrated the canopy enough to illuminate some webs but not all. Marla kept a wary eye out as they progressed to drier ground. A creature slithered into the shrubbery to their left, making her scurry past.

"Vicki Sweetwater is making a claim on her daughter's behalf." Dalton scratched his arm. The mosquitoes wouldn't abate until a cold front came to town.

"Vicki and Bill never married, so is her claim legit?" Marla asked, hoping Rose would gain some inheritance. It seemed only right.

"Vicki has a good lawyer. She and Tom can duke it out. While they both had motives, they didn't kill Bill Ripari."

"No, Jules did it to protect his friend. Mr. Ripari had been hitting on Patrick, whom he was supposed to be tutoring. The dirty old man," Marla added with a grimace.

"What's going to happen to the football coach?" Brianna asked.

"I suppose he'll be fired. Plus, he may face charges for feeding steroids to his team." Marla glanced at the teenager. "Maybe we should send you to a private school with better supervision."

Dalton placed a soothing hand on Marla's arm. "It'll be safer now with everything out in the open. The teacher's killer is in custody, and the rotten apples will be weeded out. Principal Underwood is sure to resign. The school board will be examining his role. He might have been acting in the school's best interest but in the wrong way."

"I guess so, and no doubt Brianna would rather remain with her friends."

"Not all of them." The teen's eyes blazed. "Andy didn't come to the Halloween party. Maya told me he had plans with Ilyssa for the night. I'd seen them together a couple of times, but he hadn't mentioned anything to me."

Marla gaped at her. "You mean, Andy is seeing someone else besides you? The rat. You don't need a guy like him, honey."

"Andy? Who's that? Did I miss something?" Dalton shot his daughter a suspicious glare.

Marla laughed. "Get used to it, *Dad*. This is merely the beginning. Your daughter is growing into a lovely young lady, and boys are starting to take notice."

"Oh, yeah? I'll have to meet them first before they can notice my girl."

"It's my life. I don't need you to interfere." Brianna lifted her chin. "Besides, I have Marla to guide me, and she made the perfect choice for a husband. I trust her judgement."

A warm glow filled her. Marla could handle teenage puppy love, as long as it didn't involve murder. With a sigh of content, she strode along, rejoicing in her family and the upcoming holidays they would celebrate together.

Author's Note

This novella is book 12.5 in the Bad Hair Day mystery series. It takes place between *Peril by Ponytail* and *Facials Can Be Fatal*. When I was invited to participate in the Happy Homicides 4: Fall into Crime anthology for the fall season, the idea came to me to write a Halloween tale. I hadn't featured this holiday before, and it would be the perfect setting for Brianna to involve Marla in a school function. What better place for a dead body to turn up than at a haunted house?

"Haunted Hair Nights" first appeared in the *Happy Homicides 4: Fall into Crime* cozy mystery anthology. This standalone edition includes a bonus chapter from my next title, *Facials Can Be Fatal*, #13 in the Bad Hair Day Mysteries.

If you enjoyed this story, please help spread the word. Here are some suggestions:

- Write an online customer review at Amazon, BN, or Goodreads. This need only be a few lines about why you liked a story, but it's incredibly important. New readers often base their choices on comments from people like you.
- Recommend my work to your reading groups, online forums, and book clubs.
- Gift a Bad Hair Day mystery to your hairstylist, nail tech, or beautician.
- Sign up for my Newsletter for updates on new releases, giveaways, and author events: http://nancyjcohen.com/newsletter/

About the Author

As a former registered nurse, Nancy J. Cohen helped people with their physical aches and pains, but she longed to soothe their troubles in a different way. The siren call of storytelling lured her from nursing into the exciting world of fiction. Wishing she could wield a curling iron with the same skill as crafting a story, she created hairdresser Marla Shore as a stylist with a nose for crime and a knack for exposing people's secrets.

Titles in the Bad Hair Day Mysteries have made the IMBA bestseller list and been selected by *Suspense Magazine* as best cozy mystery. Nancy is also the author of *Writing the Cozy Mystery*, a valuable instructional guide on how to write a winning whodunit. Her imaginative romances, including the Drift Lords series, have proven popular with fans as well.

A featured speaker at libraries, conferences, and community events, Nancy is listed in *Contemporary Authors, Poets & Writers*, and *Who's Who in U.S. Writers, Editors, & Poets*. When not busy writing, she enjoys fine dining, cruising, visiting Disney World, and shopping. Contact her at nancy@nancyjcohen.com

<><><>

Follow Nancy Online

Website: http://nancyjcohen.com
Blog: http://nancyjcohen.wordpress.com
Facebook: https://www.facebook.com/NancyJCohenAuthor
Twitter: http://www.twitter.com/nancyjcohen
Goodreads: http://bit.ly/9VZtEH
Pinterest: http://pinterest.com/njcohen/
Linked In: http://www.linkedin.com/in/nancyjcohen

Books by Nancy J. Cohen

Bad Hair Day Mysteries
Permed to Death
Hair Raiser
Murder by Manicure
Body Wave
Highlights to Heaven
Died Blonde
Dead Roots
Perish by Pedicure
Killer Knots
Shear Murder
Hanging by a Hair
Peril by Ponytail
Facials Can Be Fatal
Hair Brained

Anthologies
Haunted Hair Nights, in the "Happy Homicides 4: Fall Into Crime" Anthology
Three Men and a Body, in the "Wicked Women Whodunit" Kensington Anthology

The Drift Lords Series
Warrior Prince
Warrior Rogue
Warrior Lord

Science Fiction Romances
Keeper of the Rings
Silver Serenade

The Light-Years Series
Circle of Light
Moonlight Rhapsody
Starlight Child

Nonfiction
Writing the Cozy Mystery

Edited by Nancy J. Cohen
Thumbs Up by Harry I. Heller (Nancy's father)
Florida Escape by Harry I. Heller

Order Now: http://amzn.to/1BYmuXE

Facials Can Be Fatal Excerpt

Here's a sneak peek at *Facials Can Be Fatal*, book #13 in the Bad Hair Day Mysteries

Chapter One

Marla was busy sorting foils at her salon station when screams pierced the morning air. She glanced up, her nerves on edge. And here the day had started so peacefully.

Nicole, one chair over, paused in the midst of cutting a client's hair. "What is that God-awful noise?" the other stylist asked.

Marla dropped the foils on her roundabout. "I don't know, but it sounds as though it's coming from our day spa next door. Maybe someone found a palmetto bug."

But as she hurried outside and across the pavement to the adjacent spa facility—a recent expansion under her ownership along with the Cut 'N Dye hair salon—she doubted those blood-curdling shrieks could be due to an insect. They sounded too shrill and terrified.

A black bird squawked and dipped over the parking lot. Along with November and the season's first cold front, the birds had returned from up north to South Florida. That wasn't a vulture portending some disaster, was it?

Inside the day spa, patrons in the waiting area stood with their cell phones lifted, taking videos for social media. Marla sped past them toward the rear, where staff members in smocks gathered. They all stared in one direction.

Traci, the receptionist, spied Marla and called out to someone beyond her range of vision. Just as abruptly as they had started, the screams stopped.

Marla reached the group huddled in front of one of their facial and waxing rooms. "What's going on?"

An aesthetician, her complexion white as her lab coat, wiped her teary eyes. "I am sorry," she said with an accent, her voice wavering. "Val was fine when I put the cream mask on her face. I only left for ten minutes to let her relax. When I returned, she didn't move and I thought she must be asleep. I did not realize at first she was not breathing."

"I've already called 911," Traci said in a quiet undertone. "The cops and medics should be here any minute."

"Your customer isn't breathing?" Marla pushed past the crowd to enter the room and administer CPR, but the sight inside made her stop mid-track.

A woman lay supine half off the table, her hands encased in cloth mitts and her mouth wide open. Her face, coated with a greenish substance, aimed a glassy stare at the ceiling. New Age music played in the background, the soothing melody an incongruence to the scene. Air-conditioning blasted cool air into the room with a citrus scent. A discarded towel lay on the floor.

"Oh. My. God." It might be too late for CPR if the woman had lain like this for longer than ten minutes. Could she have suffered a seizure? Her bluish lips could indicate anything.

Marla forced herself to at least palpate for a pulse at the lady's neck. She tamped down the bile in her throat at the clammy feel of her skin. The hardened face mask gave the lady an almost alien appearance. Was that consistency normal for a facial?

Not feeling a beat at the carotid, Marla backed away. The

best thing she could do would be to secure the room until the cops arrived.

She swallowed uneasily, anticipating her husband's reaction. Would Dalton, a homicide detective with the Palm Haven police force, arrive on the scene when he heard the address from the dispatcher? From previous experience, she knew that unattended deaths were investigated. That would apply in this case since the aesthetician had left the client alone.

Returning to the corridor, she drew the sobbing woman aside. "What's your name?" she said, her brain foggy under the circumstances. Consuelo? Magdalena? It hovered on her tongue.

"Rosana Hernandez. Do you think she had a heart attack, *senora*? Val might have been trying to get up and call for help." Her gaze misty with tears, Rosana bent her head.

"Yes, you could be right. Had you done a medical survey on her?"

Rosana, a couple of inches shorter than Marla's five feet six, nodded. "*Si*. Val had been with me for years. She followed me when I came here from my last salon in east Fort Lauderdale. She did not have any history of heart problems or other sicknesses."

"So you've known her for quite some time." Marla glanced inside the room and grimaced. "What are those things on her hands?"

Rosana drew a deep breath. "I was giving the lady a paraffin treatment. She had a manicure scheduled next. I don't know how this could have happened."

Stomping footsteps drew their attention. The other staff members parted like the Red Sea under Moses' command. A pair of uniformed rescue workers headed their way carrying a load of equipment. Following at their heels were two patrol officers and a tall, broad-shouldered fellow whose piercing gaze made Marla's heart flutter.

She exchanged glances with Dalton but avoided embracing him in front of the staff, even when she wanted nothing more than to sink into his arms.

"I'm glad you're here," she told the EMTs. "The patient is in that room. I don't think you'll be able to do much for her."

A quick examination on their part confirmed her assessment. Dalton and one of the uniformed cops entered the room while the other officer began questioning onlookers.

"What happened?" Dalton asked Marla, tucking his cell phone away as he rejoined her. He must have made a call from inside the room.

"Rosana was giving her customer a facial. She put on the woman's face mask and left the room for a few minutes. When she returned, the lady wasn't breathing."

"Can I speak with Rosana somewhere private?"

"Sure. How come you're here? Did you recognize the address from the dispatcher?"

"That's right. Good guess." The corners of his mouth lifted. This was far from the first time he'd been summoned to her place of business.

"We can use one of the empty massage rooms," Rosana suggested in a weak tone.

Marla introduced the aesthetician to her husband. She patted the woman's shoulder. "It'll be all right. Dalton will ask you some questions, and then you can take the rest of the day off. Traci will notify your clients."

Dalton pulled out a notebook and pen and followed Rosana into another treatment room. Marla joined them, intending to offer moral support to her staff member. To her gratitude, Dalton didn't object. But then, he'd come to value her contributions. He had even identified her as his unofficial sidekick to an Arizona sheriff during their recent honeymoon.

"Okay, can you please tell me exactly what happened?" he asked Rosana.

Her lower lip trembled. "I was giving Val a facial. She has been my customer for years, and we never had a problem before."

"Her full name is...?"

"Valerie Weston. She lives east on the Intracoastal. Anyway, when I took the job here, Val followed me to this salon even though it was distant for her."

"So you've given her facials before. And she's never had a bad reaction?"

"No, sir." Rosana gave a visible shudder. "Everything was fine. I put the facial mask on, set the timer for ten minutes, and left the room so she could relax. I went to get a cup of coffee. When I returned, I found her... like that." Her voice choked on a sob, and she covered her face with her hands.

"Rosana, why don't you make a copy of your client's medical survey for Detective Vail?" Marla suggested.

"*Si*, I get it now." The white-coated woman shuffled from the room like a condemned prisoner on her way to execution.

Marla's heart went out to her. She knew how horrible Rosana felt. She'd been in the same position of losing a client when crabby Mrs. Kravitz died in the midst of getting a perm. The image of her head lolling against the shampoo sink remained with Marla even now. How many years ago had that awful incident occurred? She'd met Dalton, the detective assigned to the case, as a result. Back then, he'd suspected her of poisoning the woman's coffee creamer.

"Won't you be reassigned?" she asked him, leaning against the treatment table. "I mean, I own this place. You have a conflict of interest here." *Same as when our neighbor was found dead in his house next door after we'd argued with him.*

"We're short-staffed this time of year. A couple of the guys requested vacation time before the holiday crush. Come here."

He held out his arms, and she rushed into them. She

leaned her head against his solid chest, her anxiety easing under his embrace.

"I'm glad you came, even if your partner takes over later. I suppose you'll order an autopsy?"

"It's normal procedure. Does the woman have any close relatives nearby?"

"I have no idea. I'd never met her myself."

"What can you tell me about Rosana? Is she an immigrant? Does she have citizenship papers?"

Marla stepped away, perturbed by his return-to-business tone. "Yes, she's from Venezuela and married an American. Rosana is very good at what she does. Her customers highly recommend her."

"What was her relationship to Valerie Weston?"

Marla spread her hands. "As Rosana said, Val was her customer, and they'd known each other for years."

Rosana approached and handed a paper to Dalton. "Here is Val's client survey."

"Thank you." He scanned the contents. "It says here Ms. Weston had a latex allergy."

"That is correct, Detective. I was always careful not to use latex products in her presence and to wash my hands before touching her."

"May I take a look?" Marla snatched the paper from his fingers.

The Confidential Consultation Card, as the survey was labeled, consisted of three sections. Marla scanned Val's responses on the general health record. Topics ranged from dietary habits to female problems, sun exposure, implants, disease listings, skin-related ailments, and medications.

She nodded at that last one. Meds could affect hair as well as skin reactions. Most people didn't think to tell their hairdressers when they started on a new drug, but certain medications could cause a stronger response to chemicals such as bleach.

According to this report, Val Weston appeared to be in good health. The next two sections regarding skin care and the beautician's analysis didn't raise any red flags.

"Was she married?" Dalton asked the beautician. "Do you know who her next of kin might be?"

"She was single. No children. I know she had a sister who died recently from breast cancer."

Dalton asked a few more questions before dismissing Rosana.

Marla walked her out. "Go home and get some rest. This wasn't your fault. Val might have had an unknown medical problem to cause her death."

Rosana sniffled. *"Gracias, senora.* It is horrible."

"I know, but the police will find out what happened."

Once the staff member had left, Marla sought her husband again. He'd been conferring with one of the other officers and broke off at her approach.

She drew him aside. "What's your theory about Val's death?" The woman's image kept replaying in her head. The glassy eyes and weird greenish tint of the facial mask became increasingly grotesque in her imagination. Her stomach lurched.

Stow it, Marla. You have to remain strong.

Dalton's gaze grew warm as he regarded her. "Could be anything. Brain hemorrhage? Aortic aneurysm? Heart arrhythmia? Who knows?" His cell phone buzzed, and he squinted at an incoming text message. "The M.E. is here. Marla, you can go back to work. I'll catch you later."

"Shouldn't I stick around to support the staff?"

"It's not necessary. I'll help the uniforms interview witnesses, and then we'll close down the day spa until we complete our investigation. I know you want to keep chaos to a minimum, so I'll tell the body removal guys to use the rear entrance."

"Thanks. That'll help." *But not by much.* "I know this

might sound harsh, but I don't need the negative publicity right now. I'm in the running for that educator position with Luxor Products, and this won't look good."

"You're right. It does sound harsh in view of a woman's death. That's unlike you, Marla." The fine lines around his mouth tightened.

She knew her husband wasn't thrilled about her accepting another job, especially one that would mean more travel. They were celebrating their one-year anniversary in a couple of weeks, and she had enough to do between work and her new family. While it was a second marriage for both her and Dalton, they'd become a tight unit in a short amount of time. Marla still felt odd as Brianna's stepmother, but the role had grown on her. The teenager needed a woman's guidance.

Still, gaining the new position meant a lot to her. She had contacted the hair product company—whom she'd worked for at a beauty trade show—to let them know she'd like to do the models' hair on any advertisements they shot in the area. They'd called back saying they had an opening for an educator and asked if she would be interested. Her affirmative response had prompted the admission that they were considering one other candidate as well. Would this incident jeopardize her chances?

At any rate, Dalton was correct. She shouldn't be thinking about herself right now. As the day spa's owner, she was ultimately responsible for Val's death. And poor Rosana. This would hang over her head. Marla should see to it that the rest of the staff didn't hold it against her.

She went from person to person, speaking to each staff member in turn and reassuring them the place wouldn't stay closed for long. Her own state of nerves wasn't as steady as she appeared. Her stomach felt increasingly queasy, and she had a strong urge to sit down before her knees folded.

Nonetheless, she took time to apologize to any clients still waiting to be interviewed. "If you're here for your hair or nails, we'll fit you in next door. Go see Robyn at the front desk. Otherwise, Traci can reschedule you for next week."

"That poor woman," one of the ladies said with a sorrowful expression. "To die in the middle of getting a facial, which is supposed to be a relaxing treatment."

"I hate them myself," retorted a young blonde. "All that steam in your face, and then they squeeze open your zits. It hurts. I don't find anything pleasurable about it."

"Rosana cares about her customers," Marla said, defending her employee. "She must be doing something right, since her appointments are almost always filled."

"She messed up this time," said Miss Sourpuss.

Marla stared the woman down. "No one can predict the sudden onset of a life-threatening medical emergency. Rosana had done a thorough assessment on her. The lady didn't have any known heart conditions."

"Maybe she had a reaction to one of the products," the other customer offered with a frown. She was a middle-aged lady with tinted auburn hair, and she wore skinny pants that belonged on a thinner woman.

"Rosana would have used the same lotions on her before," Marla replied in a patient tone. "Val had been a long-term customer."

"Val, as in Valerie? That wasn't Valerie Weston, was it?" Redhead gaped at her.

"Yes, it was, although the police detective will urge you to keep this information quiet. They have yet to notify next of kin." Marla pressed her lips together. Gossip would be bad enough, but they didn't need rumors flying along with videos.

"I have tickets to her fancy ball next month. I hope they don't cancel."

Marla had a sudden sneaking suspicion that made the hairs on her nape rise. "What ball do you mean?"

"The annual holiday fundraiser for Friends of Old Florida. It's a historic building preservation society. They do the best party, especially with Yolanda Whipp showcasing her latest fashion designs. I can't wait to see what she's come up with this year."

Marla's heart sank. The dead woman had been *the* Valerie Weston? Oh, no. Putting two and two together, she slapped a hand to her mouth. Val's demise in her day spa would have more repercussions than she'd thought. What would this mean for the fashion show?

She'd been hired, along with her stylists, to do the hair of the models backstage at the highly anticipated event that took place during FOFL's annual gala. Why hadn't she recognized the connection earlier?

Because I'd been upset. Val's death threw me for a loop. And it hadn't been Val who'd hired her team. Marla's contact had been someone else from the group.

Dear Lord, this was much worse than she'd anticipated.

Stunned by her new knowledge, she addressed Traci once she was free. The receptionist's usual calm had given way to a frazzled exterior as she tapped at the computer keys to change people's appointments. This was Wednesday. Marla hoped they'd be allowed to reopen by next week.

"Tell me, did Ms. Weston show any signs of trouble when she checked in earlier?"

Traci shook her head, her shoulder-length layers framing a face that looked pale in contrast to her sangria lipstick. "She seemed fine. I liked her. Val always had a pleasant smile and something upbeat to say."

"Do you know if she had any relatives nearby?"

"Just a sister who died recently. She called FOFL her family. That's Friends of Old Florida, an organization where she devoted her time. Somebody from there made her appointment for today."

"Oh, really? Can you give me their number?"

Traci squinted at the computer as she retrieved the data. "Here it is." She wrote it down on a scrap of paper, while

Marla wondered if it could be the same person who'd hired her staff for the fashion show.

"Do you remember the person's name who called? So you're saying it wasn't Val?"

"That's correct. Sorry, I don't remember much else."

"Male or female?"

Traci's shoulders lifted and lowered. "Could have been anyone. I field a lot of calls every day."

"Okay, please let me know if anything else comes to mind."

"There is one more thing. Patty didn't come in to work today. I've called her cell a few times, but it goes straight to voice mail."

They had hair stations here for backup when the salon got too full. Patty, the shampoo assistant, helped with cleanup and other assorted tasks. She should have come in today.

"That's odd. Didn't we just hire her?"

"She's only been here two weeks. She applied when our last girl had an accident on her bike, remember?"

"And you don't have any other contact number?"

"Nope."

"That's not good. She should call in if she can't make it to work." Marla shoved the scrap of paper into her skirt pocket. "After you settle things here, why don't you take the rest of today off? Tomorrow, you can work with us at the salon. Robyn could use the extra help. And thanks for your quick action. You did good calling 911 right away."

Not wanting to keep her own customers waiting any longer, Marla hurried next door. She'd have liked to tell Dalton her latest revelations, but he was busy. And if he stayed on the case, it would mean a late night for him.

She drew in a shaky breath as she entered her salon. The bright lights, familiar sounds, and chemical scents calmed her. No matter what her problems, she needed to keep her cool and get through her appointments for the day. Customers relied upon her.

Plastering a smile on her face, she approached Robyn and gave her the rundown in a low voice so others wouldn't overhear. To her credit, Robyn gave her a reassuring grin.

"We'll do fine, Marla. Your eleven o'clock is waiting. I told her you'd been delayed, but she didn't mind."

"Now I'm off schedule. Thanks, Robyn. I'll tell you more later." She'd been lucky to hire the marketing expert after Robyn had been laid off from her corporate job. They'd become good friends aside from work.

Nicole intercepted her in the backroom where she went to mix her customer's highlights solution. Shelves of bottles and boxes faced her as she selected the proper products and then brought them over to the sink. After double-checking her client's profile card, she grabbed a bowl and began measuring components.

"So what happened? Who was screaming? I saw all the flashing lights outside." Nicole pursed her lips and leaned against a counter. The dark-skinned stylist looked svelte in a maxi-dress with a matching sweater wrap.

"You'll never believe it. Rosana, the aesthetician, was giving her customer a facial. She applied the mask and left the room for a few minutes. When she returned, the lady was dead."

"What? How?"

Marla paused to think things through. "Dalton said it could have been anything from a heart attack to a brain aneurysm. The only problem that showed up on Val's medical survey was a latex allergy, but Rosana knew this. Val had been her client for years, when she'd worked in east Fort Lauderdale."

Nicole folded her arms across her chest. "So I gather the spa will be closed for a few days?"

"Yes, but I hope we'll be able to reopen by next week. I told Traci to send all their hair and nail people over here today. Are you between clients now?"

"I'm waiting on a touch-up." The stylist glanced at her watch. "Ten more minutes."

"Traci will help Robyn tomorrow at the front desk," Marla said. "We're bound to be busier if she shifts some of the spa appointments to the salon."

"Careful, hon, you don't want to add that 30 volume bleach."

"Oops, I guess I'm more rattled than I thought." She retrieved the correct item and added it to her bowl. Her hand shook as she mixed the chemicals with a brush.

"You need to calm down."

"I can't. We have to handle the overflow. But that's not the worst of it. The woman who died was Valerie Weston from Friends of Old Florida."

"So? What does that mean?"

"FOFL is the group that hired us to do the hair at their fashion show in a few weeks. I don't want to lose that gig." She didn't mention her educator opportunity, not wishing to spring this news on her staff until it was a done deal. It would mean more hours away from the salon.

"But was this client someone you recognized? Is she the person who spoke to you about doing the show?"

"No, it was somebody else." Marla put down her brush and spared a glance her way. "Lora Larue contacted me. She's one of the board members."

"So you don't know how this Valerie was connected to the group?"

"Not really. I hope they don't blame us and cancel our contract."

"You're jumping to conclusions. How can it be our fault? That woman might have dropped dead anywhere if she'd had a true medical emergency."

"Rosana left her unattended for a brief interval. Otherwise, she might have called for help sooner." Visions of a lawsuit entered her mind. Oh, God. Marla clutched her stomach.

"Hey, come here. Give me a hug." Nicole strode forward

to embrace her and pat her on the back. "We'll be okay. Things will get back to normal."

Marla sprang away, grasping the bowl and brush before the moisture behind her eyes turned into a waterfall. "I know. And I appreciate your support, as always."

She didn't express her misgivings about the negative publicity affecting her personal goals. But she wasn't to be let off the hook so easily. Her customer, displeased at having to wait for her appointment, demanded Marla relate the whole story. She gave an abbreviated version, aware of listening ears around the salon. Her rendition left out any mention of the dead woman's medical history.

"Have you heard of this organization?" Marla asked, hoping to gain some information. She knew pitifully little about the group for whom her staff had been hired. Her fingers moved automatically to section off a strand of hair, place the foil under it, brush on the solution, and fold the foil over.

"Sorry, I haven't. How's that husband of yours, dear? Won't next month be one year you'll be married?"

"That's right," she said. "Our anniversary is December eighth."

"Any little ones in the barn yet?"

"Excuse me?"

"Are you planning on having children?"

"Dalton already has a teenage daughter. She's taking driving lessons. That's enough anxiety for us, thank you."

The woman's dark eyes met hers in the mirror. "You're young yet. You can still get pregnant. I'm sure you'd make a great mother."

All right, we need to change the subject. "Let's discuss you instead. Weren't you about to go on vacation when I saw you last?"

Marla skillfully steered the conversation away from her personal life. What concern was it to others if she and Dalton

Facials Can Be Fatal

meant to expand their family? With her past history, she didn't want children of her own. She had enough to do without the added responsibilities and constant worry. Besides, she looked forward to traveling, something she hadn't had much time to pursue on her busy career path.

While she worked, part of her mind kept track of the cop cars coming and going outside, along with the scudding clouds overhead that heralded another cold front. It wasn't until later in the afternoon that most of the police vans had left.

The body must be long gone by now, she thought, signaling for her next client to get shampooed. She was still behind schedule, but she'd catch up. And keeping busy prevented her from thinking too hard about what was happening next door. How long would it take before the autopsy results came in? She'd feel more vindicated if the woman had died from natural causes that couldn't have been prevented or treated. Would Rosana quit her job there? Or if not, would she still want to work in that room?

"Hey, Marla." Robyn approached her station, a friendly smile on her face. "There's a sales rep here to see you from Luxor Products. Shall I send her over while your customer is getting washed?"

"Luxor Products? Oh, no!" She gulped. "I mean, yes, please send her on back. I have a few minutes free."

Dear Lord. Luxor was the company where she hoped to work as an educator. Was this person truly a sales rep or someone come to evaluate her? If the latter, she was doomed.

Order Now at http://amzn.to/2aWG1PD

CPSIA information can be obtained at www.ICGtesting.com
Printed in the USA
BVOW04s1744161016
465181BV00012B/155/P